C210

 CW00938147

The Diam

2 0 JUL 2024		

The Diamond Lens
and Other Stories

Fitz-James O'Brien

Published by Hesperus Press Limited
28 Mortimer Street, London W1W 7RD
www.hesperuspress.com

This collection first published by Hesperus Press Limited, 2012
Introduction and notes © Peter Orford, 2012
Selection © Hesperus Press Limited, 2012

Designed and typeset by Fraser Muggeridge studio
Printed in Jordan by Jordan National Press

ISBN: 978-1-84391-358-0

CONTENTS

Introduction   vii

The Diamond Lens   1
The Wondersmith   35
What Was It? A Mystery   81

Notes   101
Biographical note   103

INTRODUCTION

Fitz-James O'Brien was a good writer; he could have been a great one. He lived life without much thought for the future and died young, the James Dean of the literary world. One of his defining characteristics both as a writer and as a man is his failure to commit: he rarely engaged in any long-term projects and those he did, such as his weekly column *The Man About Town* (1857), or his serial fiction *From Hand to Mouth* (1858), were cut short when he grew tired of them, often with little warning. *From Hand to Mouth* had to be completed by the editor of the paper in which it was appearing. After O'Brien's death there was talk of the great novel he had mentioned writing, but no such work has ever materialised and his canon is consequently a collection of short pieces of a widely varied style – for in addition to his own tendency to chop and change, O'Brien also frequently catered to his audience's tastes. Consequently, his works encompass poems, observational columns, melodrama, sensation fiction, literary and dramatic criticism, sentimental tales and politically fuelled articles, all written for the journals of the time, as well as a handful of plays. Today he is remembered for the supernatural short stories he wrote, in particular the three collected in this edition.

In life, as in his fiction, O'Brien packed a lively tale into a short space. It is a tale divided into four disparate chapters: a child in Ireland, a playboy in London, a bohemian in America and a soldier in the Civil War. He was born in County Cork in 1828, the son of James O'Brien, a county coroner, and Elizabeth Driscoll, whose wealthy father had no male heirs save for young Fitz-James. After her husband's death (when Fitz-James would have been around eleven years old),

Elizabeth married Decourcy O'Grady, a man of good ancestry and property. In this idyllic and well-provided life, the juvenile O'Brien made his first attempts at writing, and, curiously enough chose political topics, such as the plight of the common man against the backdrop of the famine and the mass emigration to America.

In 1849 O'Brien turned twenty-one, and with his coming of age he entered the second chapter of his life. He received his inheritance from his grandfather, believed to be worth £8,000 (approximately £600,000 in today's currency), and moved to London where he lived extravagantly and spent the entire inheritance in just two and a half years. It may have been his lack of funds that prompted him to then move to America in 1852, though once again there are rumours of an alternative explanation, including one, neither proved nor disproved, that he was involved with the wife of a soldier and sought to escape her returning husband. Whatever the reason, when O'Brien entered the third chapter of his life in the New World, he was fortunate to have literary connections formed by articles he had written in England.He settled in New York, writing for magazines and journals, and it is the output produced there for which he became celebrated in his lifetime. His final chapter then began with the start of the American Civil War. He enlisted in the Union Army in 1861 and rose to the rank of lieutenant. Shot in action in February 1862, the severity of his wounds was misdiagnosed and he died of tetanus that April. He was thirty-three years old.

O'Brien had a self-destructive personality. A popular man, with many friends in the industry, he was nonetheless said to have a fiery temper and throughout his life he got into a number of fights, disputes and narrowly-avoided duels. His lifestyle was bohemian; he gathered debts, often reaching a point of desperation before getting another article published, only to then spend the money on extravagances. O'Brien was an eleventh-hour writer, and the fact that he made a successful career out of this is both to his credit and a sign of weakness: friends spoke of his tendency to write stories or poems in one sitting, suggesting a fertile imagination that could have produced longer masterpieces if only it were coupled with discipline. It was also noted by observers that O'Brien did little revision to his work; the quality of some of his stories is therefore to his merit given that they may well be first drafts, but for every good story he produced there is another that would have benefited from a little polishing. Furthermore, critics accused him of plagiarism (and not always unjustly); the pressures of producing new work on a regular basis involved O'Brien borrowing inspiration from around him, including his own life: several of his pieces have an author as prot-agonist, while other minor details crop up, such as a minor character in *The Lost Room* (1858) being given the surname of O'Brien's grandfather. It is therefore important to place the cries of plagiarism in the context of an author who absorbed ideas and adapted them when trying to produce work at the hectic frequency required to make a living in writing.

O'Brien also often catered to popular taste, quite sensibly given that each work had to be accepted by the publishers in order for him to get paid, and in doing this he adapted his style depending on the type of work he was writing (his biographer Francis Wolle called him a 'Literary Bohemian', but it is appropriate to call him a literary chameleon too); this meant not only that he lacked his own inimitable style, which in turn makes it difficult to identify all of his stories accurately given the practice of journals to publish anonymously, but also that he was often reviewed in comparison with other writers.

Today he is most frequently likened to Edgar Allen Poe for his macabre and surreal imagination, though Wolle astutely pointed out that O'Brien's distinction from Poe was his grounding of his weird and wonderful stories in the recognisable and mundane surroundings of the contemporary world, often identifying actual New York streets and addresses as the location for extraordinary tales.

The Diamond Lens (1858) is widely considered to be O'Brien's best work. It caused a literary storm on its first publication, and from that moment forward he would always be known or introduced as 'the author of *The Diamond Lens*'. The celebration of this work was not universal; early critics accused O'Brien of stealing the idea from his rival William North, though this was robustly discredited both at the time and since; yet more recently it has been suggested more convincingly by Neil Cornwell that there are similarities between the work and an earlier tale, *TheSylph*, written by Vladimir Odoevsky in 1837. Whatever its origins, O'Brien's telling of the tale is masterfully done, the protagonist drawing us in initially with an amicable narrative of his early life, before the decline of his morals and humanity which holds the reader's attention while distancing us from what first appeared to be a rational human being.

The science fiction elements in *The Wondersmith* (1859) are less explicit than the other tales in this collection. Scholars have suggested the mannequins created by Herr Hippe are early examples of robots; where O'Brien's tale differs from another well-cited tale, E.T.A. Hoffman's *The Sandman* (1816), is that the Wondersmith's robots do not make any pretence to humanity but are distinguished precisely by their lack of it. This is not a tale to invite philosophical discussion of life, but rather a rollicking sensationalist story that revels in the horrors of the unknown. And yet, surprisingly, in the character of Solon and his romance with the Wondersmith's daughter, it provides a happy antithesis to the tragic tale of a far more famous fictional hunchback, Quasimodo, and his doomed love for Esmerelda; O'Brien's tale, while preaching the terror of a different life form, simultaneously champions the rights of a man to be loved for who he is, not how he appears.

Finally, in *What Was It?* (1859), we have what is now a recognisable type of monster in the invisible creature. At the time O'Brien was something of a pioneer, preceding by over two decades other tales of invisible creatures such as Guy de Maupassant's *The Horla* (1886), Ambrose Bierce's *The Damned Thing* (1898) and, of course, H.G. Wells's *The Invisible Man* (1897). What particularly marks O'Brien's tale out as science fiction, rather than horror, is not the monster, but the heroes' reaction to it. Their attempt to explain and understand the unknown through the use of scientific methods grounds the supernatural in the world of technology, the unreal in the realm of the possible. It was his most popular work after *The Diamond Lens*, another great success for O'Brien in his lifetime, and yet curiously, when he himself planned a collection of his works (that was ultimately not produced), this tale was not on the list of twenty he proposed. It was, however, included in the collected works printed after his death by his friend William Winter and has continued to be celebrated as one of his best ever since.

O'Brien's contemporary Charles Dickens was frequently disgruntled when others presumed that writing was an easy task, because it overlooked the time and effort he put in to shaping and perfecting his works. Fitz-James O'Brien is the other side of the coin. A great talent, O'Brien, like Dickens, produced a number of works both fictional and non-fictional for the mid-nineteenth-century press; but where Dickens strived almost fanatically to get his writing and characters just right, O'Brien's approach was altogether more human. He was a man who worked to live, not lived to work. As a person he is perhaps easier to identify with because of this, but as a writer this presents a lack of focus, which results in some good works and a lot more that have flashes of brilliance but are let down by hasty production and little to no revision. In this context, the continued interest of science fiction scholars in O'Brien's writing has been both a blessing and a curse. It has guaranteed that these stories and others remain in the public conscious-ness, when they could have easily been forgotten, and O'Brien along with them; simultaneously, it has pigeonholed him in one genre. Yet there is no doubt that the works in this collection deserve to be remembered as his best, for reasons beyond their significance to science fiction. The fantastical element of these stories showcases O'Brien's fertile imagina-tion, one of his greatest qualities as a writer. Furthermore, in each one he builds tension expertly, commanding our atten-tion; he intersperses horror with humour; he showcases his wider reading through several references and allusions, and teases out metaphysical questions while simultaneously producing a dramatic plotline. He is not the greatest writer ever to have lived, but he was a writer who lived greatly; reading these tales, which show the quality he was capable of when everything came together, it becomes apparent that with a little less decadence and a little more dedication, O'Brien could have been one of the best.

The Diamond Lens

From a very early period of my life the entire bent of my inclinations had been towards microscopic investigations. When I was not more than ten years old, a distant relative of our family, hoping to astonish my inexperience, constructed a simple microscope for me, by drilling in a disk of copper a small hole, in which a drop of pure water was sustained by capillary attraction. This very primitive apparatus, magnifying some fifty diameters, presented, it is true, only indistinct and imperfect forms, but still sufficiently wonderful to work up my imagination to a preternatural state of excitement.

Seeing me so interested in this rude instrument, my cousin explained to me all that he knew about the principles of the microscope, related to me a few of the wonders which had been accomplished through its agency, and ended by promising to send me one regularly constructed, immediately on his return to the city. I counted the days, the hours, the minutes, that intervened between that promise and his departure.

Meantime I was not idle. Every transparent substance that bore the remotest semblance to a lens I eagerly seized upon and employed in vain attempts to realise that instrument, the theory of whose construction I as yet only vaguely comprehended. All panes of glass containing those oblate spheroidal knots familiarly known as 'bull's eyes'[1] were ruthlessly destroyed, in the hope of obtaining lenses of marvellous power. I even went so far as to extract the crystalline humour from the eyes of fishes and animals, and endeavoured to press it into the microscopic service. I plead guilty to having stolen the glasses from my Aunt Agatha's spectacles, with a dim idea of grinding them into lenses of wondrous magnifying properties,– in which attempt it is scarcely necessary to say that I totally failed.

At last the promised instrument came. It was of that order known as Field's simple microscope, and had cost perhaps about fifteen dollars. As far as educational purposes went, a better apparatus could not have been selected. Accompanying it was a small treatise on the microscope,– its history, uses, and discoveries. I comprehended then for the first time the 'Arabian Nights' Entertainments'. The dull veil of ordinary existence that hung across the world seemed suddenly to roll away, and to lay bare a land of enchantments. I felt towards my companions as the seer might feel towards the ordinary masses of men. I held conversations with Nature in a tongue which they could not understand. I was in daily communication with living wonders, such as they never imagined in their wildest visions. I penetrated beyond the external portal of things, and roamed through the sanctuaries. Where they beheld only a drop of rain slowly rolling down the window-glass, I saw a universe of beings animated with all the passions common to physical life, and convulsing their minute sphere with struggles as fierce and protracted as those of men. In the common spots of mould, which my mother, good housekeeper that she was, fiercely scooped away from her jam pots, there abode for me, under the name of mildew, enchanted gardens, filled with dells and avenues of the densest foliage and most astonishing verdure, while from the fantastic boughs of these microscopic forests hung strange fruits glittering with green and silver and gold.

It was no scientific thirst that at this time filled my mind. It was the pure enjoyment of a poet to whom a world of wonders has been disclosed. I talked of my solitary pleasures to none. Alone with my microscope, I dimmed my sight, day after day and night after night poring over the marvels which it unfolded to me. I was like one who, having discovered the ancient Eden still existing in all its primitive glory, should resolve to enjoy it in solitude, and never betray to mortal the secret of its locality. The rod of my life was bent at this moment. I destined myself to be a microscopist.

Of course, like every novice, I fancied myself a discoverer. I was ignorant at the time of the thousands of acute intellects engaged in the same pursuit as myself, and with the advantages of instruments a thousand times more powerful than mine. The names of Leeuwenhoek, Williamson, Spencer, Ehrenberg, Schultz, Dujardin, Schacht, and Schleiden[2] were then entirely unknown to me, or if known, I was ignorant of their patient and wonderful researches. In every fresh specimen of Cryptogamia which I placed beneath my instrument I believed that I discovered wonders of which the world was as yet ignorant. I remember well the thrill of delight and admiration that shot through me the first time that I discovered the common wheel animalcule (*Rotifera vulgaris*) expanding and contracting its flexible spokes, and seemingly rotating through the water. Alas! as I grew older, and obtained some works treating of my favourite study, I found that I was only on the threshold of a science to the investigation of which some of the greatest men of the age were devoting their lives and intellects.

As I grew up, my parents, who saw but little likelihood of anything practical resulting from the examination of bits of moss and drops of water through a brass tube and a piece of glass, were anxious that I should choose a profession. It was their desire that I should enter the counting-house of my uncle, Ethan Blake, a prosperous merchant, who carried on business in New York. This suggestion I decisively combated. I had no taste for trade; I should only make a failure; in short, I refused to become a merchant.

5

But it was necessary for me to select some pursuit. My parents were staid New England people, who insisted on the necessity of labour; and therefore, although, thanks to the bequest of my poor Aunt Agatha, I should, on coming of age, inherit a small fortune sufficient to place me above want, it was decided, that, instead of waiting for this, I should act the nobler part, and employ the intervening years in rendering myself independent.

After much cogitation I complied with the wishes of my family, and selected a profession. I determined to study medicine at the New York Academy. This disposition of my future suited me. A removal from my relatives would enable me to dispose of my time as I pleased, without fear of detection. As long as I paid my Academy fees, I might shirk attending the lectures, if I chose; and as I never had the remotest intention of standing an examination, there was no danger of my being 'plucked'. Besides, a metropolis was the place for me. There I could obtain excellent instruments, the newest publications, intimacy with men of pursuits kindred to my own,– in short, all things necessary to ensure a profitable devotion of my life to my beloved science. I had an abundance of money, few desires that were not bounded by my illuminating mirror on one side and my object-glass on the other; what, therefore, was to prevent my becoming an illustrious investigator of the veiled worlds? It was with the most buoyant hopes that I left my New England home and established myself in New York.

THE LONGING OF A MAN OF SCIENCE

My first step, of course, was to find suitable apartments. These I obtained, after a couple of days' search, in Fourth Avenue; a very pretty second-floor unfurnished, containing sitting-room, bedroom, and a smaller apartment which I intended to fit up as a laboratory. I furnished my lodgings simply, but rather elegantly, and then devoted all my energies to the adornment of the temple of my worship. I visited Pike, the celebrated optician, and passed in review his splendid collection of microscopes,– Field's Compound, Higham's, Spencer's, Nachet's Binocular (that founded on the principles of the stereoscope), and at length fixed upon that form known as Spencer's Trunnion Microscope, as combining the greatest number of improvements with an almost perfect freedom from tremor. Along with this I purchased every possible accessory,– draw-tubes, micrometers, a *camera-lucida*, lever-stage, achromatic condensers, white cloud illuminators, prisms, parabolic condensers, polarising apparatus, forceps, aquatic boxes, fishing-tubes, with a host of other articles, all of which would have been useful in the hands of an experienced microscopist, but, as I afterwards discovered, were not of the slightest present value to me. It takes years of practice to know how to use a complicated microscope. The optician looked suspiciously at me as I made these wholesale purchases. He evidently was uncertain whether to set me down as some scientific celebrity or a madman. I think he inclined to the latter belief. I suppose I was mad. Every great genius is mad upon the subject in which he is greatest. The unsuccessful madman is disgraced, and called a lunatic.

Mad or not, I set myself to work with a zeal which few scientific students have ever equalled. I had everything to learn relative to the delicate study upon which I had embarked,– a study involving the most earnest patience, the most rigid analytic powers, the steadiest hand, the most untiring eye, the most refined and subtle manipulation.

For a long time half my apparatus lay inactively on the shelves of my laboratory, which was now most amply furnished with every possible contrivance for facilitating my investigations. The fact was that I did not know how to use some of my scientific accessories– never having been taught microscopics– and those whose use I understood theoretically were of little avail, until by practice I could attain the necessary delicacy of handling. Still, such was the fury of my ambition, such the untiring perseverance of my experiments, that, difficult to credit as it may be, in the course of one year I became theoretically and practically an accomplished microscopist.

During this period of my labours, in which I submitted specimens of every substance that came under my observation to the action of my lenses, I became a discoverer,– in a small way, it is true, for I was very young, but still a discoverer. It was I who destroyed Ehrenberg's theory that the *Volcox globator* was an animal, and proved that his 'monads' with stomachs and eyes were merely phases of the formation of a vegetable cell, and were, when they reached their mature state, incapable of the act of conjugation, or any true generative act, without which no organism rising to any stage of life higher than vegetable can be said to be complete. It was I who resolved the singular problem of rotation in the cells and hairs of plants into ciliary attraction, in spite of the assertions of Mr. Wenham and others, that my explanation was the result of an optical illusion.[3]

But notwithstanding these discoveries, laboriously and painfully made as they were, I felt horribly dissatisfied. At every step I found myself stopped by the imperfections of my instruments. Like all active microscopists, I gave my imagination full play. Indeed, it is a common complaint against many such, that they supply the defects of their instruments with the creations of their brains. I imagined depths beyond depths in Nature which the limited power of my lenses prohibited me from exploring. I lay awake at night constructing imaginary microscopes of immeasurable power, with which I seemed to pierce through all the envelopes of matter down to its original atom. How I cursed those imperfect mediums which necessity through ignorance compelled me to use! How I longed to discover the secret of some perfect lens whose magnifying power should be limited only by the resolvability of the object, and which at the same time should be free from spherical and chromatic aberrations, in short from all the obstacles over which the poor microscopist finds himself continually stumbling! I felt convinced that the simple microscope, composed of a single lens of such vast yet perfect power, was possible of construction. To attempt to bring the compound microscope up to such a pitch would have been commencing at the wrong end; this latter being simply a partially successful endeavour to remedy those very defects of the simple instrument, which, if conquered, would leave nothing to be desired.

It was in this mood of mind that I became a constructive microscopist. After another year passed in this new pursuit, experimenting on every imaginable substance,– glass, gems, flints, crystals, artificial crystals formed of the alloy of various vitreous materials,– in short, having constructed as many varieties of lenses as Argus had eyes,[4] I found myself precisely

9

where I started, with nothing gained save an extensive know-ledge of glass-making. I was almost dead with despair. My parents were surprised at my apparent want of progress in my medical studies, (I had not attended one lecture since my arrival in the city,) and the expenses of my mad pursuit had been so great as to embarrass me very seriously.

I was in this frame of mind one day, experimenting in my laboratory on a small diamond,– that stone, from its great refracting power, having always occupied my attention more than any other,– when a young Frenchman, who lived on the floor above me, and who was in the habit of occasionally visiting me, entered the room.

I think that Jules Simon was a Jew. He had many traits of the Hebrew character: a love of jewellery, of dress, and of good living. There was something mysterious about him. He always had something to sell, and yet went into excellent society. When I say sell, I should perhaps have said peddle; for his operations were generally confined to the disposal of single articles,– a picture, for instance, or a rare carving in ivory, or a pair of duelling-pistols, or the dress of a Mexican *caballero*. When I was first furnishing my rooms, he paid me a visit, which ended in my purchasing an antique silver lamp, which he assured me was a Cellini,– it was handsome enough even for that,– and some other knick-knacks for my sitting-room. Why Simon should pursue this petty trade I never could imagine. He apparently had plenty of money, and had the *entrée* of the best houses in the city,– taking care, however, I suppose, to drive no bargains within the enchanted circle of the Upper Ten.[5] I came at length to the conclusion that this peddling was but a mask to cover some greater object, and even went so far as to believe my young acquaintance to be implicated in the slave-trade. That, however, was none of my affair.

On the present occasion, Simon entered my room in a state of considerable excitement.

'*Ah! mon ami!*' he cried, before I could even offer him the ordinary salutation, 'it has occurred to me to be the witness of the most astonishing things in the world. I promenade myself to the house of Madame– How does the little animal– *le renard* – name himself in the Latin?'

'Vulpes,' I answered.

'Ah! yes,– Vulpes. I promenade myself to the house of Madame Vulpes.'

'The spirit medium?'

'Yes, the great medium. Great Heavens! What a woman! I write on a slip of paper many of questions concerning affairs the most secret,– affairs that conceal themselves in the abysses of my heart the most profound; and behold! By example! What occurs? This devil of a woman makes me replies the most truthful to all of them. She talks to me of things that I do not love to talk of to myself. What am I to think? I am fixed to the earth!'

'Am I to understand you, M. Simon, that this Mrs. Vulpes replied to questions secretly written by you, which questions related to events known only to yourself?'

'Ah! more than that, more than that,' he answered, with an air of some alarm. 'She related to me things– But,' he added, after a pause, and suddenly changing his manner, 'why occupy ourselves with these follies? It was all the Biology, without doubt. It goes without saying that it has not my credence.But why are we here, *mon ami*? It has occurred to me to discover the most beautiful thing as you can imagine,– a vase with green lizards on it, composed by the great Bernard Palissy. It is in my apartment; let us mount. I go to show it to you.'

I followed Simon mechanically; but my thoughts were far from Palissy and his enamelled ware, although I, like him, was seeking in the dark after a great discovery. This casual mention of the spiritualist, Madame Vulpes, set me on a new track. What if this spiritualism should be really a great fact? What if, through communication with subtler organisms than my own, I could reach at a single bound the goal, which perhaps a life of agonising mental toil would never enable me to attain?

While purchasing the Palissy vase from my friend Simon, I was mentally arranging a visit to Madame Vulpes.

III
THE SPIRIT OF LEEUWENHOEK

Two evenings after this, thanks to an arrangement by letter and the promise of an ample fee, I found Madame Vulpes awaiting me at her residence alone. She was a coarse-featured woman, with a keen and rather cruel dark eye, and an exceedingly sensual expression about her mouth and under jaw. She received me in perfect silence, in an apartment on the ground floor, very sparsely furnished. In the centre of the room, close to where Mrs. Vulpes sat, there was a common round mahogany table. If I had come for the purpose of sweeping her chimney, the woman could not have looked more indifferent to my appearance. There was no attempt to inspire the visitor with any awe. Everything bore a simple and practical aspect. This intercourse with the spiritual world was evidently as familiar an occupation with Mrs. Vulpes as eating her dinner or riding in an omnibus.

'You come for a communication, Mr. Linley?' said the medium, in a dry, business-like tone of voice.

'By appointment,– yes.'

'What sort of communication do you want? A written one?'

'Yes,– I wish for a written one.'

'From any particular spirit?'

'Yes.'

'Have you ever known this spirit on this earth?'

'Never. He died long before I was born. I wish merely to obtain from him some information which he ought to be able to give better than any other.'

'Will you seat yourself at the table, Mr. Linley,' said the medium, 'and place your hands upon it?'

I obeyed,– Mrs. Vulpes being seated opposite me, with her hands also on the table. We remained thus for about a minute and a half, when a violent succession of raps came on the table, on the back of my chair, on the floor immediately under my feet, and even on the window-panes. Mrs. Vulpes smiled composedly.

'They are very strong tonight,' she remarked. 'You are fortunate.' She then continued, 'Will the spirits communicate with this gentleman?'

Vigorous affirmative.

'Will the particular spirit he desires to speak with communicate?'

A very confused rapping followed this question.

'I know what they mean,' said Mrs. Vulpes, addressing herself to me; 'they wish you to write down the name of the particular spirit that you desire to converse with. Is that so?' she added, speaking to her invisible guests.

That it was so was evident from the numerous affirmatory responses. While this was going on, I tore a slip from my pocket-book, and scribbled a name under the table.

'Will this spirit communicate in writing with this gentleman?' asked the medium once more.

After a moment's pause her hand seemed to be seized with a violent tremor, shaking so forcibly that the table vibrated. She said that a spirit had seized her hand and would write. I handed her some sheets of paper that were on the table, and a pencil. The latter she held loosely in her hand, which presently began to move over the paper with a singular and seemingly involuntary motion. After a few moments had elapsed she handed me the paper, on which I found written, in a large, uncultivated hand, the words, 'He is not here, but has been sent for.' A pause of a minute or so now ensued, during which Mrs. Vulpes remained perfectly silent, but the raps continued at regular intervals. When the short period I mention had elapsed, the hand of the medium was again seized with its convulsive tremor, and she wrote, under this strange influence, a few words on the paper, which she handed to me. They were as follows:–

'I am here. Question me.'

'LEEUWENHOEK.'

I was astounded. The name was identical with that I had written beneath the table, and carefully kept concealed. Neither was it at all probable that an uncultivated woman like Mrs. Vulpes should know even the name of the great father of microscopics. It may have been Biology; but this theory was soon doomed to be destroyed. I wrote on my slip– still concealing it from Mrs. Vulpes– a series of questions, which, to avoid tediousness, I shall place with the responses in the order in which they occurred.

I.– Can the microscope be brought to perfection?
SPIRIT.– Yes.

I.– Am I destined to accomplish this great task?

SPIRIT.– You are.

I.– I wish to know how to proceed to attain this end. For the love which you bear to science, help me!

SPIRIT.– A diamond of one hundred and forty carats, submitted to electromagnetic currents for a long period, will experience a rearrangement of its atoms *inter se*, and from that stone you will form the universal lens.

I.– Will great discoveries result from the use of such a lens?

SPIRIT.– So great, that all that has gone before is as nothing.

I.– But the refractive power of the diamond is so immense, that the image will be formed within the lens. How is that difficulty to be surmounted?

SPIRIT.– Pierce the lens through its axis, and the difficulty is obviated. The image will be formed in the pierced space, which will itself serve as a tube to look through. Now I am called. Good night!

I cannot at all describe the effect that these extraordinary communications had upon me. I felt completely bewildered. No biological theory could account for the *discovery* of the lens. The medium might, by means of biological *rapport* with my mind, have gone so far as to read my questions, and reply to them coherently. But Biology could not enable her to discover that magnetic currents would so alter the crystals of the diamond as to remedy its previous defects, and admit of its being polished into a perfect lens. Some such theory may have passed through my head, it is true; but if so, I had forgotten it. In my excited condition of mind there was no course left but to become a convert, and it was in a state of the most painful nervous exaltation that I left the medium's house that evening. She accompanied me to the door, hoping that I was satisfied. The raps followed us as we went through the hall, sounding on the balusters, the flooring, and even the lintels of the door. I hastily expressed my satisfaction, and escaped hurriedly into the cool night air. I walked home with but one thought possessing me,– how to obtain a diamond of the immense size required. My entire means multiplied a hundred times over would have been inadequate to its purchase. Besides, such stones are rare, and become historical. I could find such only in the regalia of Eastern or European monarchs.

IV
THE EYE OF MORNING

There was a light in Simon's room as I entered my house. A vague impulse urged me to visit him. As I opened the door of his sitting-room unannounced, he was bending, with his back toward me, over a carcel lamp,[6] apparently engaged in minutely examining some object which he held in his hands. As I entered, he started suddenly, thrust his hand into his breast pocket, and turned to me with a face crimson with confusion.

'What!' I cried, 'poring over the miniature of some fair lady? Well, don't blush so much; I won't ask to see it.'

Simon laughed awkwardly enough, but made none of the negative protestations usual on such occasions. He asked me to take a seat.

'Simon,' said I, 'I have just come from Madame Vulpes.'

This time Simon turned as white as a sheet, and seemed stupefied, as if a sudden electric shock had smitten him. He babbled some incoherent words, and went hastily to a small closet where he usually kept his liquors. Although astonished at his emotion, I was too preoccupied with my own idea to pay much attention to anything else.

'You say truly when you call Madame Vulpes a devil of a woman,' I continued. 'Simon, she told me wonderful things tonight, or rather was the means of telling me wonderful things. Ah! If I could only get a diamond that weighed one hundred and forty carats!'

Scarcely had the sigh with which I uttered this desire died upon my lips, when Simon, with the aspect of a wild beast, glared at me savagely, and rushing to the mantel-piece, where some foreign weapons hung on the wall, caught up a Malay creese,[7] and brandished it furiously before him.

'No!' he cried in French, into which he always broke when excited. 'No! you shall not have it! You are perfidious! You have consulted with that demon, and desire my treasure! But I will die first! Me! I am brave! You cannot make me fear!'

All this, uttered in a loud voice trembling with excitement, astounded me. I saw at a glance that I had accidentally trodden upon the edges of Simon's secret, whatever it was. It was necessary to reassure him.

'My dear Simon,' I said, 'I am entirely at a loss to know what you mean. I went to Madame Vulpes to consult with her on a scientific problem, to the solution of which I discovered that a diamond of the size I just mentioned was necessary. You were never alluded to during the evening, nor, so far as I was concerned, even thought of. What can be the meaning of this outburst? If you happen to have a set of valuable diamonds in your possession, you need fear nothing from me. The diamond which I require you could not possess; or if you did possess it, you would not be living here.'

Something in my tone must have completely reassured him; for his expression immediately changed to a sort of constrained merriment, combined, however, with a certain suspicious attention to my movements. He laughed, and said that I must bear with him; that he was at certain moments subject to a species of vertigo, which betrayed itself in incoherent speeches, and that the attacks passed off as rapidly as they came. He put his weapon aside while making this explanation, and endeavoured, with some success, to assume a more cheerful air.

All this did not impose on me in the least. I was too much accustomed to analytical labours to be baffled by so flimsy a veil. I determined to probe the mystery to the bottom.

'Simon,' I said, gaily, 'let us forget all this over a bottle of Burgundy. I have a case of Lausseure's *Clos Vougeot* downstairs, fragrant with the odours and ruddy with the sunlight of the Cote d'Or. Let us have up a couple of bottles. What say you?'

'With all my heart,' answered Simon, smilingly.

I produced the wine and we seated ourselves to drink. It was of a famous vintage, that of 1848, a year when war and wine throve together,– and its pure, but powerful juice seemed to impart renewed vitality to the system. By the time we had half finished the second bottle, Simon's head, which I knew was a weak one, had begun to yield, while I remained calm as ever, only that every draught seemed to send a flush of vigour through my limbs. Simon's utterance became more and more indistinct. He took to singing French *chansons* of a not very moral tendency. I rose suddenly from the table just at the conclusion of one of those incoherent verses, and fixing my eyes on him with a quiet smile, said:

'Simon, I have deceived you. I learned your secret this evening. You may as well be frank with me. Mrs. Vulpes, or rather, one of her spirits, told me all.'

He started with horror. His intoxication seemed for the moment to fade away, and he made a movement towards the weapon that he had a short time before laid down. I stopped him with my hand.

'Monster!' he cried, passionately, 'I am ruined! What shall I do? You shall never have it! I swear by my mother!'

'I don't want it,' I said; 'rest secure, but be frank with me. Tell me all about it.'

The drunkenness began to return. He protested with maudlin earnestness that I was entirely mistaken,– that I was intoxicated; then asked me to swear eternal secrecy, and promised to disclose the mystery to me. I pledged myself, of course, to all. With an uneasy look in his eyes, and hands unsteady with drink and nervousness, he drew a small case from his breast and opened it. Heavens! How the mild lamp-light was shivered into a thousand prismatic arrows, as it fell upon a vast rose-diamond that glittered in the case! I was no judge of diamonds, but I saw at a glance that this was a gem of rare size and purity. I looked at Simon with wonder, and – must I confess it?– with envy. How could he have obtained this treasure? In reply to my questions, I could just gather from his drunken statements (of which, I fancy, half the incoherence was affected) that he had been superintending a gang of slaves engaged in diamond-washing in Brazil; that he had seen one of them secrete a diamond, but, instead of informing his employers, had quietly watched the negro until he saw him bury his treasure; that he had dug it up, and fled with it, but that as yet he was afraid to attempt to dispose of it publicly,– so valuable a gem being almost certain to attract too much attention to its owner's antecedents,– and he had not been able to discover any of those obscure channels by which such matters are conveyed away safely. He added that, in accordance with Oriental practice, he had named his diamond by the fanciful title of 'The Eye of Morning.'

While Simon was relating this to me, I regarded the great diamond attentively. Never had I beheld anything so beautiful. All the glories of light, ever imagined or described, seemed to pulsate in its crystalline chambers. Its weight, as I learned from Simon, was exactly one hundred and forty carats. Here was an amazing coincidence. The hand of Destiny seemed in it. On the very evening when the spirit of Leeuwenhoek communicates to me the great secret of the microscope, the priceless means which he directs me to employ start up within my reach! I determined, with the most perfect deliberation, to possess myself of Simon's diamond.

I sat opposite him while he nodded over his glass, and calmly revolved the whole affair. I did not for an instant contemplate so foolish an act as a common theft, which would of course be discovered, or at least necessitate flight and concealment, all of which must interfere with my scientific plans. There was but one step to be taken,– to kill Simon. After all, what was the life of a little peddling Jew, in comparison with the interests of science? Human beings are taken every day from the condemned prisons to be experimented on by surgeons. This man, Simon, was by his own confession a criminal, a robber, and I believed on my soul a murderer. He deserved death quite as much as any felon condemned by the laws; why should I not, like government, contrive that his punishment should contribute to the progress of human knowledge?

The means for accomplishing everything I desired lay within my reach. There stood upon the mantelpiece a bottle half full of French laudanum. Simon was so occupied with his diamond, which I had just restored to him, that it was an affair of no difficulty to drug his glass. In a quarter of an hour he was in a profound sleep.

I now opened his waistcoat, took the diamond from the inner pocket in which he had placed it, and removed him to the bed, on which I laid him so that his feet hung down over the edge. I had possessed myself of the Malay creese, which I held in my right hand, while with the other I discovered as accurately as I could by pulsation the exact locality of the heart. It was essential that all the aspects of his death should lead to the surmise of self-murder. I calculated the exact angle at which it was probable that the weapon, if levelled by Simon's own hand, would enter his breast; then with one powerful blow I thrust it up to the hilt in the very spot which I desired to penetrate. A convulsive thrill ran through Simon's limbs. I heard a smothered sound issue from his throat, precisely like the bursting of a large air-bubble, sent up by a diver, when it reaches the surface of the water; he turned half round on his side, and as if to assist my plans more effectually, his right hand, moved by some mere spasmodic impulse, clasped the handle of the creese, which it remained holding with extraordinary muscular tenacity. Beyond this there was no apparent struggle. The laudanum, I presume, paralysed the usual nervous action. He must have died instantaneously.

There was yet something to be done. To make it certain that all suspicion of the act should be diverted from any inhabitant of the house to Simon himself, it was necessary that the door should be found in the morning *locked on the inside*. How to do this, and afterwards escape myself? Not by the window; that was a physical impossibility. Besides, I was determined that the windows *also* should be found bolted. The solution was simple enough. I descended softly to my own room for a peculiar instrument which I had used for holding small slippery substances, such as minute spheres of glass, etc. This instrument was nothing more than a long slender hand-vice, with a very powerful grip, and a considerable leverage, which last was accidentally owing to the shape of the handle. Nothing was simpler than, when the key was in the lock, to seize the end of its stem in this vice, through the keyhole, from the outside, and so lock the door. Previously, however, to doing this, I burned a number of papers on Simon's hearth. Suicides almost always burn papers before they destroy themselves. I also emptied some more laudanum into Simon's glass,– having first removed from it all traces of wine,– cleaned the other wine-glass, and brought the bottle away with me. If traces of two persons drinking had been found in the room, the question naturally would have arisen, who was the second? Besides, the wine-bottle might have been identified as belonging to me. The laudanum I poured out to account for its presence in his stomach, in case of a *post-mortem* examination. The theory naturally would be, that he first intended to poison himself, but, after swallowing a little of the drug, was either disgusted with its taste, or changed his mind from other motives, and chose the dagger. These arrangements made, I walked out, leaving the gas burning, locked the door with my vice, and went to bed.

Simon's death was not discovered until nearly three in the afternoon. The servant, astonished at seeing the gas burning,– the light streaming on the dark landing from under the door,– peeped through the keyhole and saw Simon on the bed. She gave the alarm. The door was burst open, and the neighbourhood was in a fever of excitement.

Everyone in the house was arrested, myself included. There was an inquest; but no clue to his death, beyond that of suicide, could be obtained. Curiously enough, he had made several speeches to his friends the preceding week, that seemed to point to self-destruction. One gentleman swore that Simon had said in his presence that 'he was tired of life'. His landlord affirmed, that Simon, when paying him his last month's rent, remarked that 'he would not pay him rent much longer'. All the other evidence corresponded,– the door locked inside, the position of the corpse, the burnt papers. As I anticipated, no one knew of the possession of the diamond by Simon, so that no motive was suggested for his murder. The jury, after a prolonged examination, brought in the usual verdict, and the neighbourhood once more settled down into its accustomed quiet.

V

ANIMULA

The three months succeeding Simon's catastrophe I devoted night and day to my diamond lens. I had constructed a vast galvanic battery, composed of nearly two thousand pairs of plates,– a higher power I dared not use, lest the diamond should be calcined.[8] By means of this enormous engine I was enabled to send a powerful current of electricity continually through my great diamond, which it seemed to me gained in lustre every day. At the expiration of a month I commenced the grinding and polishing of the lens, a work of intense toil and exquisite delicacy. The great density of the stone, and the care required to be taken with the curvatures of the surfaces of the lens, rendered the labour the severest and most harassing that I had yet undergone.

At last the eventful moment came; the lens was completed. I stood trembling on the threshold of new worlds. I had the realisation of Alexander's famous wish before me.[9] The lens lay on the table, ready to be placed upon its platform. My hand fairly shook as I enveloped a drop of water with a thin coating of oil of turpentine, preparatory to its examination,– a process necessary in order to prevent the rapid evaporation of the water. I now placed the drop on a thin slip of glass under the lens, and throwing upon it, by the combined aid of a prism and a mirror, a powerful stream of light, I approached my eye to the minute hole drilled through the axis of the lens. For an instant I saw nothing save what seemed to be an illuminated chaos, a vast luminous abyss. A pure white light, cloudless and serene, and seemingly limitless as space itself, was my first impression. Gently, and with the greatest care, I depressed the lens a few hairs' breadths. The wondrous illumination still continued, but as the lens approached the object, a sense of indescribable beauty was unfolded to my view.

I seemed to gaze upon a vast space, the limits of which extended far beyond my vision. An atmosphere of magical luminousness permeated the entire field of view. I was amazed to see no trace of animalculous life. Not a living thing, apparently, inhabited that dazzling expanse. I comprehended instantly, that, by the wondrous power of my lens, I had penetrated beyond the grosser particles of aqueous matter, beyond the realms of Infusoria and Protozoa, down to the original gaseous globule, into whose luminous interior I was gazing, as into an almost boundless dome filled with a super-natural radiance.

It was, however, no brilliant void into which I looked. On every side I beheld beautiful inorganic forms, of unknown texture, and coloured with the most enchanting hues. These forms presented the appearance of what might be called, for want of a more specific definition, foliated clouds of the highest rarity; that is, they undulated and broke into vegetable formations, and were tinged with splendours compared with which the gilding of our autumn woodlands is as dross compared with gold. Far away into the illimitable distance stretched long avenues of these gaseous forests, dimly transparent, and painted with prismatic hues of unimaginable brilliancy. The pendent branches waved along the fluid glades until every vista seemed to break through half-lucent ranks of many-coloured drooping silken pennons. What seemed to be either fruits or flowers, pied with a thousand hues lustrous and ever varying, bubbled from the crowns of this fairy foliage. No hills, no lakes, no rivers, no forms animate or inanimate were to be seen, save those vast auroral copses that floated serenely in the luminous stillness, with leaves and fruits and flowers gleaming with unknown fires, unrealisable by mere imagination.

How strange, I thought, that this sphere should be thus condemned to solitude! I had hoped, at least, to discover some new form of animal life,– perhaps of a lower class than any with which we are at present acquainted,– but still, some living organism. I find my newly discovered world, if I may so speak, a beautiful chromatic desert.

While I was speculating on the singular arrangements of the internal economy of Nature, with which she so frequently splinters into atoms our most compact theories, I thought I beheld a form moving slowly through the glades of one of the prismatic forests. I looked more attentively, and found that I was not mistaken. Words cannot depict the anxiety with which I awaited the nearer approach of this mysterious object. Was it merely some inanimate substance, held in suspense in the attenuated atmosphere of the globule? Or was it an animal endowed with vitality and motion? It approached, flitting behind the gauzy, coloured veils of cloud-foliage, for seconds dimly revealed, then vanishing. At last the violet pennons that trailed nearest to me vibrated; they were gently pushed aside, and the Form floated out into the broad light.

It was a female human shape. When I say 'human', I mean it possessed the outlines of humanity,– but there the analogy ends. Its adorable beauty lifted it illimitable heights beyond the loveliest daughter of Adam.

I cannot, I dare not, attempt to inventory the charms of this divine revelation of perfect beauty. Those eyes of mystic violet, dewy and serene, evade my words. Her long lustrous hair following her glorious head in a golden wake, like the track sown in heaven by a falling star, seems to quench my most burning phrases with its splendours. If all the bees of Hybla nestled upon my lips, they would still sing but hoarsely the wondrous harmonies of outline that enclosed her form.

She swept out from between the rainbow-curtains of the cloud-trees into the broad sea of light that lay beyond. Her motions were those of some graceful Naiad, cleaving, by a mere effort of her will, the clear, unruffled waters that fill the chambers of the sea. She floated forth with the serene grace of a frail bubble ascending through the still atmosphere of a June day. The perfect roundness of her limbs formed suave and enchanting curves. It was like listening to the most spiritual symphony of Beethoven the divine, to watch the harmonious flow of lines. This, indeed, was a pleasure cheaply purchased at any price. What cared I, if I had waded to the portal of this wonder through another's blood? I would have given my own to enjoy one such moment of intoxication and delight.

Breathless with gazing on this lovely wonder, and forgetful for an instant of everything save her presence, I withdrew my eye from the microscope eagerly,–alas! As my gaze fell on the thin slide that lay beneath my instrument, the bright light from mirror and from prism sparkled on a colourless drop of water! There, in that tiny bead of dew, this beautiful being was forever imprisoned. The planet Neptune was not more distant from me than she. I hastened once more to apply my eye to the microscope.

Animula (let me now call her by that dear name which I subsequently bestowed on her) had changed her position. She had again approached the wondrous forest, and was gazing earnestly upwards. Presently one of the trees – as I must call them – unfolded a long ciliary process, with which it seized one of the gleaming fruits that glittered on its summit, and sweeping slowly down, held it within reach of Animula. The sylph took it in her delicate hand, and began to eat. My attention was so entirely absorbed by her, that I could not apply myself to the task of determining whether this singular plant was or was not instinct with volition.

I watched her, as she made her repast, with the most profound attention. The suppleness of her motions sent a thrill of delight through my frame; my heart beat madly as she turned her beautiful eyes in the direction of the spot in which I stood. What would I not have given to have had the power to precipitate myself into that luminous ocean, and float with her through those groves of purple and gold! While I was thus breathlessly following her every movement, she suddenly started, seemed to listen for a moment, and then cleaving the brilliant ether in which she was floating, like a flash of light, pierced through the opaline forest, and disappeared.

Instantly a series of the most singular sensations attacked me. It seemed as if I had suddenly gone blind. The luminous sphere was still before me, but my daylight had vanished. What caused this sudden disappearance? Had she a lover, or a husband? Yes, that was the solution! Some signal from a happy fellow-being had vibrated through the avenues of the forest, and she had obeyed the summons.

The agony of my sensations, as I arrived at this conclusion, startled me. I tried to reject the conviction that my reason forced upon me. I battled against the fatal conclusion,– but in vain. It was so. I had no escape from it. I loved an animalcule!

It is true, that, thanks to the marvellous power of my microscope, she appeared of human proportions. Instead of presenting the revolting aspect of the coarser creatures, that live and struggle and die, in the more easily resolvable portions of the water-drop, she was fair and delicate and of surpassing beauty. But of what account was all that? Every time that my eye was withdrawn from the instrument, it fell on a miserable drop of water, within which, I must be content to know, dwelt all that could make my life lovely.

Could she but see me once! Could I for one moment pierce the mystical walls that so inexorably rose to separate us, and whisper all that filled my soul, I might consent to be satisfied for the rest of my life with the knowledge of her remote sympathy. It would be something to have established even the faintest personal link to bind us together,– to know that at times, when roaming through those enchanted glades, she might think of the wonderful stranger, who had broken the monotony of her life with his presence, and left a gentle memory in her heart!

But it could not be. No invention, of which human intellect was capable, could break down the barriers that Nature had erected. I might feast my soul upon her wondrous beauty, yet she must always remain ignorant of the adoring eyes that day and night gazed upon her, and, even when closed, beheld her in dreams. With a bitter cry of anguish I fled from the room, and, flinging myself on my bed, sobbed myself to sleep like a child.

VI
THE SPILLING OF THE CUP

I arose the next morning almost at daybreak, and rushed to my microscope. I trembled as I sought the luminous world in miniature that contained my all. Animula was there. I had left the gas-lamp, surrounded by its moderators, burning, when I went to bed the night before. I found the sylph bathing, as it were, with an expression of pleasure animating her features, in the brilliant light which surrounded her. She tossed her lustrous golden hair over her shoulders with innocent coquetry. She lay at full length in the transparent medium, in which she supported herself with ease, and gambolled with the enchanting grace that the Nymph Salmacis might have exhibited when she sought to conquer the modest Hermaphroditus.[10] I tried an experiment to satisfy myself if her powers of reflection were developed. I lessened the lamp-light considerably. By the dim light that remained, I could see an expression of pain flit across her face. She looked upward suddenly, and her brows contracted. I flooded the stage of the microscope again with a full stream of light, and her whole expression changed. She sprang forward like some substance deprived of all weight. Her eyes sparkled, and her lips moved. Ah! if science had only the means of conducting and reduplicating sounds, as it does the rays of light, what carols of happiness would then have entranced my ears! what jubilant hymns to Adonaïs would have thrilled the illumined air!

I now comprehended how it was that the Count de Gabalis peopled his mystic world with sylphs,– beautiful beings whose breath of life was lambent fire, and who sported forever in regions of purest ether and purest light. The Rosicrucian had anticipated the wonder that I had practically realised.[11]

How long this worship of my strange divinity went on thus I scarcely know. I lost all note of time. All day from early dawn, and far into the night, I was to be found peering through that wonderful lens. I saw no one, went nowhere, and scarce allowed myself sufficient time for my meals. My whole life was absorbed in contemplation as rapt as that of any of the Romish saints. Every hour that I gazed upon the divine form strengthened my passion,– a passion that was always overshadowed by the maddening conviction, that, although I could gaze on her at will, she never, never could behold me!

At length I grew so pale and emaciated, from want of rest, and continual brooding over my insane love and its cruel conditions, that I determined to make some effort to wean myself from it. 'Come,' I said, 'this is at best but a fantasy. Your imagination has bestowed on Animula charms which in reality she does not possess. Seclusion from female society has produced this morbid condition of mind. Compare her with the beautiful women of your own world, and this false enchantment will vanish.'

I looked over the newspapers by chance. There I beheld the advertisement of a celebrated *danseuse* who appeared nightly at Niblo's. The Signorina Caradolce had the reputation of being the most beautiful as well as the most graceful woman in the world. I instantly dressed and went to the theatre.

The curtain drew up. The usual semi-circle of fairies in white muslin were standing on the right toe around the enamelled flower-bank, of green canvas, on which the belated prince was sleeping. Suddenly a flute is heard. The fairies start. The trees open, the fairies all stand on the left toe, and the queen enters. It was the Signorina. She bounded forward amid thunders of applause, and lighting on one foot remained poised in air. Heavens! was this the great enchantress that had drawn monarchs at her chariot-wheels? Those heavy muscular limbs, those thick ankles, those cavernous eyes, that stereo-typed smile, those crudely painted cheeks! Where were the vermeil blooms, the liquid expressive eyes, the harmonious limbs of Animula?

The Signorina danced. What gross, discordant movements! The play of her limbs was all false and artificial. Her bounds were painful athletic efforts; her poses were angular and distressed the eye. I could bear it no longer; with an exclama-tion of disgust that drew every eye upon me, I rose from my seat in the very middle of the Signorina's *pas-de-fascination*, and abruptly quitted the house.

I hastened home to feast my eyes once more on the lovely form of my sylph. I felt that henceforth to combat this passion would be impossible. I applied my eye to the lens. Animula was there,– but what could have happened? Some terrible change seemed to have taken place during my absence. Some secret grief seemed to cloud the lovely features of her I gazed upon. Her face had grown thin and haggard; her limbs trailed heavily; the wondrous lustre of her golden hair had faded. She was ill! – ill, and I could not assist her! I believe at that moment I would have gladly forfeited all claims to my human birthright, if I could only have been dwarfed to the size of an animalcule, and per-mitted to console her from whom fate had forever divided me.

I racked my brain for the solution of this mystery. What was it that affected the sylph? She seemed to suffer intense pain. Her features contracted, and she even writhed, as if with some internal agony. The wondrous forests appeared also to have lost half their beauty. Their hues were dim and in some places faded away altogether. I watched Animula for hours with a breaking heart, and she seemed absolutely to wither away under my very eye. Suddenly I remembered that I had not looked at the water-drop for several days. In fact, I hated to see it; for it reminded me of the natural barrier between Animula and myself. I hurriedly looked down on the stage of the microscope. The slide was still there,– but, great heavens! the water-drop had vanished! The awful truth burst upon me; it had evaporated, until it had become so minute as to be invisible to the naked eye; I had been gazing on its last atom, the one that contained Animula,– and she was dying!

I rushed again to the front of the lens, and looked through. Alas! the last agony had seized her. The rainbow-hued forests had all melted away, and Animula lay struggling feebly in what seemed to be a spot of dim light. Ah! the sight was horrible: the limbs once so round and lovely shrivelling up into nothings; the eyes– those eyes that shone like heaven– being quenched into black dust; the lustrous golden hair now lank and discoloured. The last throe came. I beheld that final struggle of the blackening form– and I fainted.

When I awoke out of a trance of many hours, I found myself lying amid the wreck of my instrument, myself as shattered in mind and body as it. I crawled feebly to my bed, from which I did not rise for months.

They say now that I am mad; but they are mistaken. I am poor, for I have neither the heart nor the will to work; all my money is spent, and I live on charity. Young men's associations that love a joke invite me to lecture on optics before them, for which they pay me, and laugh at me while I lecture. 'Linley, the mad microscopist,' is the name I go by. I suppose that I talk incoherently while I lecture. Who could talk sense when his brain is haunted by such ghastly memories, while ever and anon among the shapes of death I behold the radiant form of my lost Animula!

The Wondersmith

I
GOLOSH STREET AND ITS PEOPLE

A small lane, the name of which I have forgotten, or do not choose to remember, slants suddenly off from Chatham Street, (before that headlong thoroughfare reaches into the Park,) and retreats suddenly down towards the East River, as if it were disgusted with the smell of old clothes, and had determined to wash itself clean. This excellent intention it has, however, evidently contributed towards the making of that imaginary pavement mentioned in the old adage; for it is still emphatically a dirty street. It has never been able to shake off the Hebraic taint of filth which it inherits from the ancestral thoroughfare. It is slushy and greasy, as if it were twin brother of the Roman Ghetto.

I like a dirty slum; not because I am naturally unclean,– I have not a drop of Neapolitan blood in my veins,– but because I generally find a certain sediment of philosophy precipitated in its gutters. A clean street is terribly prosaic. There is no food for thought in carefully swept pavements, barren kennels, and vulgarly spotless houses. But when I go down a street which has been left so long to itself that it has acquired a distinct outward character, I find plenty to think about. The scraps of sodden letters lying in the ash-barrel have their meaning: desperate appeals, perhaps, from Tom, the baker's assistant, to Amelia, the daughter of the dry-goods retailer, who is always selling at a sacrifice in consequence of the late fire. That may be Tom himself who is now passing me in a white apron, and I look up at the windows of the house (which does not, however, give any signs of a recent conflagration) and almost hope to see Amelia wave a white pocket-handkerchief. The bit of orange-peel lying on the sidewalk inspires thought. Who will fall over it? Who but the industrious mother of six children, the eldest of which is only nine months old, all of whom are dependent on her exertions for support? I see her slip and tumble. I see the pale face convulsed with agony, and the vain struggle to get up; the pitying crowd closing her off from all air; the anxious young doctor who happened to be passing by; the manipulation of the broken limb, the shake of the head, the moan of the victim, the litter borne on men's shoulders, the gates of the New York Hospital unclosing, the subscription taken up on the spot. There is some food for speculation in that three-year-old, tattered child, masked with dirt, who is throwing a brick at another three-year-old, tattered child, masked with dirt. It is not difficult to perceive that he is destined to lurk, as it were, through life. His bad, flat face– or, at least, what can be seen of it– does not look as if it were made for the light of day. The mire in which he wallows now is but a type of the moral mire in which he will wallow hereafter. The feeble little hand lifted at this instant to smite his companion, half in earnest, half in jest, will be raised against his fellow-beings forevermore.

Golosh Street– as I will call this nameless lane before alluded to– is an interesting locality. All the oddities of trade seem to have found their way thither and made an eccentric mercantile settlement. There is a bird-shop at one corner, wainscoted with little cages containing linnets, waxwings, canaries, blackbirds, mino-birds, with a hundred other varieties, known only to naturalists. Immediately opposite is an establishment where they sell nothing but ornaments made out of the tinted leaves of autumn, varnished and gummed into various forms. Farther down is a second-hand book-stall, which looks like a sentry-box mangled out flat, and which is remarkable for not containing a complete set of any work.

There is a small chink between two ordinary-sized houses, in which a little Frenchman makes and sells artificial eyes, specimens of which, ranged on a black velvet cushion, stare at you unwinkingly through the window as you pass, until you shudder and hurry on, thinking how awful the world would be, if everyone went about without eyelids. There are junk-shops in Golosh Street that seem to have got hold of all the old nails in the Ark and all the old brass of Corinth. Madame Filomel, the fortune-teller, lives at No. 12 Golosh Street, second story front, pull the bell on the left-hand side. Next door to Madame is the shop of Herr Hippe, commonly called the Wondersmith.

Herr Hippe's shop is the largest in Golosh Street, and to all appearance is furnished with the smallest stock. Beyond a few packing-cases, a turner's lathe, and a shelf laden with dissected maps of Europe, the interior of the shop is entirely unfur-nished. The window, which is lofty and wide, but much begrimed with dirt, contains the only pleasant object in the place. This is a beautiful little miniature theatre,–that is to say, the orchestra and stage. It is fitted with charmingly painted scenery and all the appliances for scenic changes. There are tiny traps, and delicately constructed 'lifts', and real footlights fed with burning-fluid, and in the orchestra sits a diminutive conductor before his desk, surrounded by musical man-nequins, all provided with the smallest of violoncellos, flutes, oboes, drums, and such like. There are characters also on the stage. A Templar in a white cloak is dragging a fainting female form to the parapet of a ruined bridge, while behind a great black rock on the left one can see a man concealed, who, kneeling, levels an arquebus at the knight's heart. But the orchestra is silent; the conductor never beats the time, the musicians never play a note. The Templar never drags his victim an inch nearer to the bridge, the masked avenger takes an eternal aim with his weapon. This repose appears unnatural; for so admirably are the figures executed, that they seem replete with life. One is almost led to believe, in looking on them, that they are resting beneath some spell which hinders their motion. One expects every moment to hear the loud explosion of the arquebus,– to see the blue smoke curling, the Templar falling,– to hear the orchestra playing the requiem of the guilty.

Few people knew what Herr Hippe's business or trade really was. That he worked at something was evident; else why the shop? Some people inclined to the belief that he was an inventor, or mechanician. His workshop was in the rear of the store, and into that sanctuary no one but himself had admission. He arrived in Golosh Street eight or ten years ago, and one fine morning, the neighbours, taking down their shutters, observed that No. 13 had got a tenant. A tall, thin, sallow-faced man stood on a ladder outside the shop-entrance, nailing up a large board, on which 'Herr Hippe, Wondersmith', was painted in black letters on a yellow ground. The little theatre stood in the window, where it stood ever after, and Herr Hippe was established.

But what was a Wondersmith? people asked each other. No one could reply. Madame Filomel was consulted, but she looked grave, and said that it was none of her business. Mr. Pippel, the bird-fancier, who was a German, and ought to know best, thought it was the English for some singular Teutonic profession; but his replies were so vague, that Golosh Street was as unsatisfied as ever. Solon, the little humpback, who kept the odd-volume book-stall at the lowest corner, could throw no light upon it. And at length people had to come to the conclusion, that Herr Hippe was either a coiner or a magician, and opinions were divided.

II
A BOTTLEFUL OF SOULS

It was a dull December evening. There was little trade doing in Golosh Street, and the shutters were up at most of the shops. Hippe's store had been closed at least an hour, and the mino-birds and Bohemian waxwings at Mr. Pippel's had their heads tucked under their wings in their first sleep.

Herr Hippe sat in his parlour, which was lit by a pleasant wood-fire. There were no candles in the room, and the flickering blaze played fantastic tricks on the pale grey walls. It seemed the festival of shadows. Processions of shapes, obscure and indistinct, passed across the leaden-hued panels and vanished in the dusk corners. Every fresh blaze flung up by the wayward logs created new images. Now it was a funeral throng, with the bowed figures of mourners, the shrouded coffin, the plumes that waved like extinguished torches; now a knightly cavalcade with flags and lances, and weird horses, that rushed silently along until they met the angle of the room, when they pranced through the wall and vanished.

On a table close to where Herr Hippe sat was placed a large square box of some dark wood, while over it was spread a casing of steel, so elaborately wrought in an open arabesque pattern that it seemed like a shining blue lace which was lightly stretched over its surface.

Herr Hippe lay luxuriously in his arm-chair, looking meditatively into the fire. He was tall and thin, and his skin was of a dull saffron hue. Long, straight hair,– sharply cut, regular features,– a long, thin moustache, that curled like a dark asp around his mouth, the expression of which was so bitter and cruel that it seemed to distil the venom of the ideal

41

serpent,– and a bony, muscular form, were the prominent characteristics of the Wondersmith.

The profound silence that reigned in the chamber was broken by a peculiar scratching at the panel of the door, like that which at the French court was formerly substituted for the ordinary knock, when it was necessary to demand admission to the royal apartments. Herr Hippe started, raised his head, which vibrated on his long neck like the head of a cobra when about to strike, and after a moment's silence uttered a strange guttural sound. The door unclosed, and a squat, broad-shouldered woman, with large, wild, Oriental eyes, entered softly.

'Ah! Filomel, you are come!' said the Wondersmith, sinking back in his chair. 'Where are the rest of them?'

'They will be here presently,' answered Madame Filomel, seating herself in an arm-chair much too narrow for a person of her proportions, and over the sides of which she bulged like a pudding.

'Have you brought the souls?' asked the Wondersmith.

'They are here,' said the fortune-teller, drawing a large pot-bellied black bottle from under her cloak. 'Ah! I have had such trouble with them!'

'Are they of the right brand,– wild, tearing, dark, devilish fellows? We want no essence of milk and honey, you know. None but souls bitter as hemlock or scorching as lightning will suit our purpose.'

'You will see, you will see, Grand Duke of Egypt![12] They are ethereal demons, every one of them. They are the pick of a thousand births. Do you think that I, old midwife that I am, don't know the squall of the demon child from that of the angel child, the very moment they are delivered? Ask a musician, how he knows, even in the dark, a note struck by Thalberg from one struck by Liszt!'

42

'I long to test them,' cried the Wondersmith, rubbing his hands joyfully. 'I long to see how the little devils will behave when I give them their shapes. Ah! it will be a proud day for us when we let them loose upon the cursed Christian children! Through the length and breadth of the land they will go; wherever our wandering people set foot, and wherever they are, the children of the Christians shall die. Then we, the despised Bohemians, the gypsies, as they call us, will be once more lords of the earth, as we were in the days when the accursed things called cities did not exist, and men lived in the free woods and hunted the game of the forest. Toys indeed! Ay, ay, we will give the little dears toys! toys that all day will sleep calmly in their boxes, seemingly stiff and wooden and without life,– but at night, when the souls enter them, will arise and surround the cots of the sleeping children, and pierce their hearts with their keen, envenomed blades! Toys indeed! oh, yes! I will sell them toys!'

And the Wondersmith laughed horribly, while the snaky moustache on his upper lip writhed as if it had truly a serpent's power and could sting.

'Have you got your first batch, Herr Hippe?' asked Madame Filomel. 'Are they all ready?'

'Oh, ay! they are ready,' answered the Wondersmith with gusto,– opening, as he spoke, the box covered with the blue steel lace-work; 'they are here.'

The box contained a quantity of exquisitely carved wooden manikins of both sexes, painted with great dexterity so as to present a miniature resemblance to Nature. They were, in fact, nothing more than admirable specimens of those toys which children delight in placing in various positions on the table,– in regiments, or sitting at meals, or grouped under the stiff green trees which always accompany them in the boxes in which they are sold at the toy-shops.

The peculiarity, however, about the manikins of Herr Hippe was not alone the artistic truth with which the limbs and the features were gifted; but on the countenance of each little puppet the carver's art had wrought an expression of wickedness that was appalling. Every tiny face had its special stamp of ferocity. The lips were thin and brimful of malice; the small black bead-like eyes glittered with the fire of a universal hate. There was not one of the manikins, male or female, that did not hold in his or her hand some miniature weapon. The little men, scowling like demons, clasped in their wooden fingers swords delicate as a housewife's needle. The women, whose countenances expressed treachery and cruelty, clutched infinitesimal daggers, with which they seemed about to take some terrible vengeance.

'Good!' said Madame Filomel, taking one of the manikins out of the box, and examining it attentively; 'you work well, Duke Balthazar! These little ones are of the right stamp; they look as if they had mischief in them. Ah! here come our brothers.'

At this moment the same scratching that preceded the entrance of Madame Filomel was heard at the door, and Herr Hippe replied with a hoarse, guttural cry. The next moment two men entered. The first was a small man with very brilliant eyes. He was wrapped in a long shabby cloak, and wore a strange nondescript species of cap on his head, such a cap as one sees only in the low billiard-rooms in Paris. His companion was tall, long-limbed, and slender; and his dress, although of the ordinary cut, either from the disposition of colours, or from the careless, graceful attitudes of the wearer, assumed a certain air of picturesqueness. Both the men possessed the same marked Oriental type of countenance which distinguished the Wondersmith and Madame Filomel.

44

True gypsies they seemed, who would not have been out of place telling fortunes, or stealing chickens in the green lanes of England, or wandering with their wild music and their sleight-of-hand tricks through Bohemian villages.

'Welcome, brothers!' said the Wondersmith; 'you are in time. Sister Filomel has brought the souls, and we are about to test them. Monsieur Kerplonne, take off your cloak. Brother Oaksmith, take a chair. I promise you some amusement this evening; so make yourselves comfortable. Here is something to aid you.'

And while the Frenchman Kerplonne, and his tall companion, Oaksmith, were obeying Hippe's invitation, he reached over to a little closet let into the wall, and took thence a squat bottle and some glasses, which he placed on the table.

'Drink, brothers!' he said; 'it is not Christian blood, but good stout wine of Oporto. It goes right to the heart, and warms one like the sunshine of the South.'

'It is good,' said Kerplonne, smacking his lips with enthusiasm.

'Why don't you keep brandy? Hang wine!' cried Oaksmith, after having swallowed two bumpers in rapid succession.

'Bah! Brandy has been the ruin of our race. It has made us sots and thieves. It shall never cross my threshold,' cried the Wondersmith, with a sombre indignation.

'A little of it is not bad, though, Duke,' said the fortune-teller. 'It consoles us for our misfortunes; it gives us the crowns we once wore; it restores to us the power we once wielded; it carries us back, as if by magic, to that land of the sun from which fate has driven us; it darkens the memory of all the evils that we have for centuries suffered.'

'It is a devil; may it be cursed!' cried Herr Hippe, passionately. 'It is a demon that stole from me my son, the finest youth in all Courland.[13] Yes! my son, the son of the Waywode Balthazar, Grand Duke of Lower Egypt, died raving in a gutter, with an empty brandy-bottle in his hands. Were it not that the plant is a sacred one to our race, I would curse the grape and the vine that bore it.'

This outburst was delivered with such energy that the three gypsies kept silence. Oaksmith helped himself to another glass of port, and the fortune-teller rocked to and fro in her chair, too much overawed by the Wondersmith's vehemence of manner to reply. The little Frenchman, Kerplonne, took no part in the discussion, but seemed lost in admiration of the manikins, which he took from the box in which they lay, handling them with the greatest care. After the silence had lasted for about a minute, Herr Hippe broke it with the sudden question,—

'How does your eye get on, Kerplonne?'

'Excellently, Duke. It is finished. I have it here.' And the little Frenchman put his hand into his breeches-pocket and pulled out a large artificial human eye. Its great size was the only thing in this eye that would lead any one to suspect its artificiality. It was at least twice the size of life; but there was a fearful speculative light in its iris, which seemed to expand and contract like the eye of a living being, that rendered it a horrible staring paradox. It looked like the naked eye of the Cyclops, torn from his forehead, and still burning with wrath and the desire for vengeance.

The little Frenchman laughed pleasantly as he held the eye in his hand, and gazed down on that huge dark pupil, that stared back at him, it seemed, with an air of defiance and mistrust.

'It is a devil of an eye,' said the little man, wiping the enamelled surface with an old silk pocket-handkerchief; 'it

46

reads like a demon. My niece – the unhappy one – has a wretch of a lover, and I have a long time feared that she would run away with him. I could not read her correspondence, for she kept her writing-desk closely locked. But I asked her yesterday to keep this eye in some very safe place for me. She put it, as I knew she would, into her desk, and by its aid I read every one of her letters. She was to run away next Monday, the ungrateful! but she will find herself disappointed.'

And the little man laughed heartily at the success of his stratagem, and polished and fondled the great eye until that optic seemed to grow sore with rubbing.

'And you have been at work, too, I see, Herr Hippe. Your manikins are excellent. But where are the souls?'

'In that bottle,' answered the Wondersmith, pointing to the pot-bellied black bottle that Madame Filomel had brought with her. 'Yes, Monsieur Kerplonne,' he continued, 'my manikins are well made. I invoked the aid of Abigor, the demon of soldiery, and he inspired me. The little fellows will be famous assassins when they are animated. We will try them tonight.'

'Good!' cried Kerplonne, rubbing his hands joyously. 'It is close upon New Year's Day. We will fabricate millions of the little murderers by New Year's Eve, and sell them in large quantities; and when the households are all asleep, and the Christian children are waiting for Santa Claus to come, the small ones will troop from their boxes and the Christian children will die. It is famous! Health to Abigor!'

'Let us try them at once,' said Oaksmith. 'Is your daughter, Zonéla, in bed, Herr Hippe? Are we secure from intrusion?'

'No one is stirring about the house,' replied the Wondersmith, gloomily.

Filomel leaned over to Oaksmith, and said, in an undertone,–

47

'Why do you mention his daughter? You know he does not like to have her spoken about.'

'I will take care that we are not disturbed,' said Kerplonne, rising. 'I will put my eye outside the door, to watch.'

He went to the door and placed his great eye upon the floor with tender care. As he did so, a dark form, unseen by him or his second vision, glided along the passage noiselessly and was lost in the darkness.

'Now for it!' exclaimed Madam Filomel, taking up her fat black bottle. 'Herr Hippe, prepare your manikins!'

The Wondersmith took the little dolls out, one by one, and set them upon the table. Such an array of villainous countenances was never seen. An army of Italian bravos, seen through the wrong end of a telescope, or a band of prisoners at the galleys in Lilliput, will give some faint idea of the appearance they presented. While Madame Filomel uncorked the black bottle, Herr Hippe covered the dolls over with a species of linen tent, which he took also from the box. This done, the fortune-teller held the mouth of the bottle to the door of the tent, gathering the loose cloth closely round the glass neck. Immediately, tiny noises were heard inside the tent. Madame Filomel removed the bottle, and the Wondersmith lifted the covering in which he had enveloped his little people.

A wonderful transformation had taken place. Wooden and inflexible no longer, the crowd of manikins were now in full motion. The beadlike eyes turned, glittering, on all sides; the thin, wicked lips quivered with bad passions; the tiny hands sheathed and unsheathed the little swords and daggers. Episodes, common to life, were taking place in every direction. Here two martial manikins paid court to a pretty sly-faced female, who smiled on each alternately, but gave her hand to be kissed to a third manikin, an ugly little scoundrel, who crouched behind her back. There a pair of friendly dolls walked arm in arm, apparently on the best terms, while, all the time, one was watching his opportunity to stab the other in the back.

'I think they'll do,' said the Wondersmith, chuckling, as he watched these various incidents. 'Treacherous, cruel, blood-thirsty. All goes marvellously well. But stay! I will put the grand test to them.'

So saying, he drew a gold dollar from his pocket, and let it fall on the table in the very midst of the throng of manikins. It had hardly touched the table when there was a pause on all sides. Every head was turned towards the dollar. Then about twenty of the little creatures rushed towards the glittering coin. One, fleeter than the rest, leaped upon it, and drew his sword. The entire crowd of little people had now gathered round this new centre of attraction. Men and women struggled and shoved to get nearer to the piece of gold. Hardly had the first Lilliputian mounted upon the treasure, when a hundred blades flashed back a defiant answer to his, and a dozen men, sword in hand, leaped upon the yellow platform and drove him off at the sword's point. Then commenced a general battle. The minia-ture faces were convulsed with rage and avarice. Each furious doll tried to plunge dagger or sword into his or her neighbour, and the women seemed possessed by a thousand devils.

'They will break themselves into atoms,' cried Filomel, as she watched with eagerness this savage *mêlée*. 'You had better gather them up, Herr Hippe. I will exhaust my bottle and suck all the souls back from them.'

'Oh, they are perfect devils! they are magnificent little demons!' cried the Frenchman, with enthusiasm. 'Hippe, you are a wonderful man. Brother Oaksmith, you have no such man as Hippe among your English gypsies.'

49

'Not exactly,' answered Oaksmith, rather sullenly, 'not exactly. But we have men there who can make a twelve-year-old horse look like a four-year-old,– and who can take you and Herr Hippe up with one hand, and throw you over their shoulders.'

'The good God forbid!' said the little Frenchman. 'I do not love such play. It is incommodious.'

While Oaksmith and Kerplonne were talking, the Wondersmith had placed the linen tent over the struggling dolls, and Madame Filomel, who had been performing some mysterious manipulations with her black bottle, put the mouth once more to the door of the tent. In an instant the confused murmur within ceased. Madame Filomel corked the bottle quickly. The Wondersmith withdrew the tent, and, lo! the furious dolls were once more wooden-jointed and inflexible; and the old sinister look was again frozen on their faces.

'They must have blood, though,' said Herr Hippe, as he gathered them up and put them into their box. 'Mr. Pippel, the bird-fancier, is asleep. I have a key that opens his door. We will let them loose among the birds; it will be rare fun.'

'Magnificent!' cried Kerplonne. 'Let us go on the instant. But first let me gather up my eye.'

The Frenchman pocketed his eye, after having given it a polish with the silk handkerchief; Herr Hippe extinguished the lamp; Oaksmith took a last bumper of port; and the four gypsies departed for Mr. Pippel's, carrying the box of manikins with them.

III
SOLON

The shadow that glided along the dark corridor, at the moment that Monsieur Kerplonne deposited his sentinel eye outside the door of the Wondersmith's apartment, sped swiftly through the passage and ascended the stairs to the attic. Here the shadow stopped at the entrance to one of the chambers and knocked at the door. There was no reply.

'Zonéla, are you asleep?' said the shadow, softly.

'Oh, Solon, is it you?' replied a sweet low voice from within. 'I thought it was Herr Hippe. Come in.'

The shadow opened the door and entered. There were neither candles nor lamp in the room; but through the projecting window, which was open, there came the faint gleams of the starlight, by which one could distinguish a female figure seated on a low stool in the middle of the floor.

'Has he left you without light again, Zonéla?' asked the shadow, closing the door of the apartment. 'I have brought my little lantern with me, though.'

'Thank you, Solon,' answered she called Zonéla; 'you are a good fellow. He never gives me any light of an evening, but bids me go to bed. I like to sit sometimes and look at the moon and the stars,– the stars more than all; for they seem all the time to look right back into my face, very sadly, as if they would say, "We see you, and pity you, and would help you, if we could." But it is so mournful to be always looking at such myriads of melancholy eyes! and I long so to read those nice books that you lend me, Solon!'

By this time the shadow had lit the lantern and was a shadow no longer. A large head, covered with a profusion of long blonde hair, which was cut after that fashion known as *à l'enfants d'Edouard*; a beautiful pale face, lit with wide, blue, dreamy eyes; long arms and slender hands, attenuated legs, and – an enormous hump;– such was Solon, the shadow. As soon as the humpback had lit the lamp, Zonéla arose from the low stool on which she had been seated, and took Solon's hand affectionately in hers.

Zonéla was surely not of gypsy blood. That rich auburn hair, that looked almost black in the lamp-light, that pale, transparent skin, tinged with an under-glow of warm rich blood, the hazel eyes, large and soft as those of a fawn, were never begotten of a Zingaro. Zonéla was seemingly about sixteen; her figure, although somewhat thin and angular, was full of the unconscious grace of youth. She was dressed in an old cotton print, which had been once of an exceedingly boisterous pattern, but was now a mere suggestion of former splendour; while round her head was twisted, in fantastic fashion, a silk handkerchief of green ground spotted with bright crimson. This strange headdress gave her an elfish appearance.

'I have been out all day with the organ, and I am so tired, Solon!– not sleepy, but weary, I mean. Poor Furbelow was sleepy, though, and he's gone to bed.'

'I'm weary, too, Zonéla;– not weary as you are, though, for I sit in my little book-stall all day long, and do not drag round an organ and a monkey and play old tunes for pennies,– but weary of myself, of life, of the load that I carry on my shoulders'; and, as he said this, the poor humpback glanced sideways, as if to call attention to his deformed person.

'Well, but you ought not to be melancholy amidst your books, Solon. Gracious! If I could only sit in the sun and read as you do, how happy I should be! But it's very tiresome to trudge round all day with that nasty organ, and look up at the houses, and know that you are annoying the people inside; and then the boys play such bad tricks on poor Furbelow, throwing him hot pennies to pick up, and burning his poor little hands; and oh! sometimes, Solon, the men in the street make me so afraid,– they speak to me and look at me so oddly! – I'd a great deal rather sit in your book-stall and read.'

'I have nothing but odd volumes in my stall,' answered the humpback. 'Perhaps that's right, though; for, after all, I'm nothing but an odd volume myself.'

'Come, don't be melancholy, Solon. Sit down and tell me a story. I'll bring Furbelow to listen.'

So saying, she went to a dusk corner of the cheerless attic-room, and returned with a little Brazilian monkey in her arms,– a poor, mild, drowsy thing, that looked as if it had cried itself to sleep. She sat down on her little stool, with Furbelow in her lap, and nodded her head to Solon, as much as to say, 'Go on; we are attentive.'

'You want a story, do you?' said the humpback, with a mournful smile. 'Well, I'll tell you one. Only what will your father say, if he catches me here?'

'Herr Hippe is not my father,' cried Zonéla, indignantly. 'He's a gypsy, and I know I'm stolen; and I'd run away from him, if I only knew where to run to. If I were his child, do you think that he would treat me as he does? make me trudge round the city, all day long, with a barrel-organ and a monkey,– though I love poor dear little Furbelow,– and keep me up in a garret, and give me ever so little to eat? I know I'm not his child, for he hates me.'

'Listen to my story, Zonéla, and we'll talk of that afterwards. Let me sit at your feet';– and, having coiled himself up at the little maiden's feet, he commenced:–

'There once lived in a great city, just like this city of New York, a poor little hunchback. He kept a second-hand book-stall, where he made barely enough money to keep body and soul together. He was very sad at times, because he knew scarce anyone, and those that he did know did not love him. He had passed a sickly, secluded youth. The children of his neighbourhood would not play with him, for he was not made like them; and the people in the streets stared at him with pity, or scoffed at him when he went by. Ah! Zonéla, how his poor heart was wrung with bitterness when he beheld the procession of shapely men and fine women that every day passed him by in the thoroughfares of the great city! How he repined and cursed his fate as the torrent of fleet-footed firemen dashed past him to the toll of the bells, magnificent in their overflowing vitality and strength! But there was one consolation left him,– one drop of honey in the jar of gall, so sweet that it ameliorated all the bitterness of life. God had given him a deformed body, but his mind was straight and healthy. So the poor hunchback shut himself into the world of books, and was, if not happy, at least contented. He kept company with courteous paladins, and romantic heroes, and beautiful women; and this society was of such excellent breeding that it never so much as once noticed his poor crooked back or his lame walk. The love of books grew upon him with his years. He was remarked for his studious habits; and when, one day, the obscure people that he called father and mother – parents only in name – died, a compassionate book-vendor gave him enough stock in trade to set up a little stall of his own. Here, in his book-stall, he sat in the sun all day, waiting for the customers that seldom came, and reading the fine deeds of the people of the ancient time, or the beautiful thoughts of the poets that had warmed millions of hearts before that hour, and still glowed for him with undiminished fire. One day, when he was reading some book, that, small as it was, was big enough to shut the whole world out from him, he heard some music in the street. Looking up from his book, he saw a little girl, with large eyes, playing an organ, while a monkey begged for alms from a crowd of idlers who had nothing in their pockets but their hands. The girl was playing, but she was also weeping. The merry notes of the polka were ground out to a silent accompaniment of tears. She looked very sad, this organ-girl, and her monkey seemed to have caught the infection, for his large brown eyes were moist, as if he also wept. The poor hunchback was struck with pity, and called the little girl over to give her a penny,– not, dear Zonéla, because he wished to bestow alms, but because he wanted to speak with her. She came, and they talked together. She came the next day,– for it turned out that they were neighbours,– and the next, and, in short, every day. They became friends. They were both lonely and afflicted, with this difference, that she was beautiful, and he – was a hunchback.'

'Why, Solon,' cried Zonéla, 'that's the very way you and I met!'

'It was then,' continued Solon, with a faint smile, 'that life seemed to have its music. A great harmony seemed to the poor cripple to fill the world. The carts that took the flour-barrels from the wharves to the store-houses seemed to emit joyous melodies from their wheels. The hum of the great business-streets sounded like grand symphonies of triumph. As one who has been travelling through a barren country without much heed feels with singular force the sterility of the lands he has passed through when he reaches the fertile plains that lie at the end of his journey, so the humpback, after his vision had been freshened with this blooming flower, remembered for the first time the misery of the life that he had led. But he did not allow himself to dwell upon the past. The present was so delightful that it occupied all his thoughts. Zonéla, he was in love with the organ-girl.'

'Oh, that's so nice!' said Zonéla, innocently,– pinching poor Furbelow, as she spoke, in order to dispel a very evident snooze that was creeping over him. 'It's going to be a love-story.'

'Ah! but, Zonéla, he did not know whether she loved him in return. You forget that he was deformed.'

'But,' answered the girl, gravely, 'he was good.'

A light like the flash of an aurora illuminated Solon's face for an instant. He put out his hand suddenly, as if to take Zonéla's and press it to his heart; but an unaccountable timidity seemed to arrest the impulse, and he only stroked Furbelow's head,– upon which that individual opened one large brown eye to the extent of the eighth of an inch, and, seeing that it was only Solon, instantly closed it again, and resumed his dream of a city where there were no organs and all the copper coin of the realm was iced.

'He hoped and feared,' continued Solon, in a low, mournful voice; 'but at times he was very miserable, because he did not think it possible that so much happiness was reserved for him as the love of this beautiful, innocent girl. At night, when he was in bed, and all the world was dreaming, he lay awake looking up at the old books that hung against the walls, thinking how he could bring about the charming of her heart. One night, when he was thinking of this, with his eyes fixed upon the mouldy backs of the odd volumes that lay on their shelves, and looked back at him wistfully, as if they would say,– 'We also are like you, and wait to be completed,'– it seemed as if he heard a rustle of leaves. Then, one by one, the books came down from their places to the floor, as if shifted by invisible hands, opened their worm-eaten covers, and from between the pages of each the hunchback saw issue forth a curious throng of little people that danced here and there through the apartment. Each one of these little creatures was shaped so as to bear resemblance to some one of the letters of the alphabet. One tall, long-legged fellow seemed like the letter A; a burly fellow, with a big head and a paunch, was the model of B; another leering little chap might have passed for a Q; and so on through the whole. These fairies – for fairies they were – climbed upon the hunchback's bed, and clustered thick as bees upon his pillow. "Come!" they cried to him, "we will lead you into fairy-land." So saying, they seized his hand, and he suddenly found himself in a beautiful country, where the light did not come from sun or moon or stars, but floated round and over and in everything like the atmosphere. On all sides he heard mysterious melodies sung by strangely musical voices. None of the features of the landscape were definite; yet when he looked on the vague harmonies of colour that melted one into another before his sight, he was filled with a sense of inexplicable beauty. On every side of him fluttered radiant bodies which darted to and fro through the illumined space. They were not birds, yet they flew like birds; and as each one crossed the path of his vision, he felt a strange delight flash through his brain, and straightway an interior voice seemed to sing beneath the vaulted dome of his temples a verse containing some beautiful thought. The little fairies were all this time dancing and fluttering around him, perching on his head, on his shoulders, or balancing themselves on his finger-tips. "Where am I?" he asked, at last, of his friends, the fairies. "Ah! Solon," he heard them whisper, in tones that sounded like the distant tinkling of silver bells, "this land is nameless;

but those whom we lead hither, who tread its soil, and breathe its air, and gaze on its floating sparks of light, are poets forevermore!" Having said this, they vanished, and with them the beautiful indefinite land, and the flashing lights, and the illumined air; and the hunchback found himself again in bed, with the moonlight quivering on the floor, and the dusty books on their shelves, grim and mouldy as ever.'

'You have betrayed yourself. You called yourself Solon,' cried Zonéla. 'Was it a dream?'

'I do not know,' answered Solon; 'but since that night I have been a poet.'

'A poet?' screamed the little organ-girl, 'a real poet, who makes verses which everyone reads and everyone talks of?'

'The people call me a poet,' answered Solon, with a sad smile. 'They do not know me by the name of Solon, for I write under an assumed title; but they praise me, and repeat my songs. But, Zonéla, I can't sing this load off of my back, can I?'

'Oh, bother the hump!' said Zonéla, jumping up suddenly. 'You're a poet, and that's enough, isn't it? I'm so glad you're a poet, Solon! You must repeat all your best things to me, won't you?'

Solon nodded assent.

'You don't ask me,' he said, 'who was the little girl that the hunchback loved.'

Zonéla's face flushed crimson. She turned suddenly away, and ran into a dark corner of the room. In a moment she returned with an old hand-organ in her arms.

'Play, Solon, play!' she cried. 'I am so glad that I want to dance. Furbelow, come and dance in honour of Solon the Poet.'

It was her confession. Solon's eyes flamed, as if his brain had suddenly ignited. He said nothing; but a triumphant smile broke over his countenance. Zonéla, the twilight of whose cheeks was still rosy with the setting blush, caught the lazy Furbelow by his little paws; Solon turned the crank of the organ, which wheezed out as merry a polka as its asthma would allow, and the girl and the monkey commenced their fantastic dance. They had taken but a few steps when the door suddenly opened, and the tall figure of the Wondersmith appeared on the threshold. His face was convulsed with rage, and the black snake that quivered on his upper lip seemed to rear itself as if about to spring upon the hunchback.

IV
THE MANIKINS AND THE MINOS

The four gypsies left Herr Hippe's house cautiously, and directed their steps towards Mr. Pippel's bird-shop. Golosh Street was asleep. Nothing was stirring in that tenebrous slum, save a dog that savagely gnawed a bone which lay on a dust-heap, tantalising him with the flavour of food without its substance. As the gypsies moved stealthily along in the darkness, they had a sinister and murderous air that would not have failed to attract the attention of the policeman of the quarter, if that worthy had not at the moment been comfortably ensconced in the neighbouring 'Rainbow' bar-room, listening to the improvisations of that talented vocalist, Mr. Harrison, who was making impromptu verses on every possible subject, to the accompaniment of a cithern which was played by a sad little Italian in a large cloak, to whom the host of the 'Rainbow' gave so many toddies and a dollar for his nightly performance.

Mr. Pippel's shop was but a short distance from the Wondersmith's house. A few moments, therefore, brought the gypsy party to the door, when, by aid of a key which Herr Hippe produced, they silently slipped into the entry. Here the Wondersmith took a dark-lantern from under his cloak, removed the cap that shrouded the light, and led the way into the shop, which was separated from the entry only by a glass door, that yielded, like the outer one, to a key which Hippe took from his pocket. The four gypsies now entered the shop and closed the door behind them.

It was a little world of birds. On every side, whether in large or small cages, one beheld balls of various-coloured feathers standing on one leg and breathing peacefully. Love-birds, nestling shoulder to shoulder, with their heads tucked under their wings and all their feathers puffed out, so that they looked like globes of malachite; English bullfinches, with ashen-coloured backs, in which their black heads were buried, and corselets of a rosy down; Java sparrows, fat and sleek and cleanly; troupials, so glossy and splendid in plumage that they looked as if they were dressed in the celebrated armour of the Black Prince, which was jet, richly damascened with gold; a cock of the rock, gleaming, a ball of tawny fire, like a setting sun; the Campanero of Brazil, white as snow, with his dilatable tolling-tube hanging from his head, placid and silent;– these, with a humbler crowd of linnets, canaries, robins, mocking-birds, and phoebes, slumbered calmly in their little cages, that were hung so thickly on the wall as not to leave an inch of it visible.

'Splendid little morsels, all of them!' exclaimed Monsieur Kerplonne. 'Ah we are going to have a rare beating!'

'So Pippel does not sleep in his shop,' said the English gypsy, Oaksmith.

'No. The fellow lives somewhere up one of the avenues,' answered Madame Filomel. 'He came, the other evening,

60

to consult me about his fortune. I did not tell him,' she added, with a laugh, 'that he was going to have so distinguished a sporting party on his premises.'

'Come,' said the Wondersmith, producing the box of manikins, 'get ready with souls, Madame Filomel. I am impatient to see my little men letting out lives for the first time.'

Just at the moment that the Wondersmith uttered this sentence, the four gypsies were startled by a hoarse voice issuing from a corner of the room, and propounding in the most guttural tones the intemperate query of 'What'll you take?' This sottish invitation had scarce been given, when a second extremely thick voice replied from an opposite corner, in accents so rough that they seemed to issue from a throat torn and furrowed by the liquid lava of many barrooms, 'Brandy and water.'

'Hollo! who's here?' muttered Herr Hippe, flashing the light of his lantern round the shop.

Oaksmith turned up his coat-cuffs, as if to be ready for a fight; Madame Filomel glided, or rather rolled, towards the door; while Kerplonne put his hand into his pocket, as if to assure himself that his supernumerary optic was all right.

'What'll you take?' croaked the voice in the corner, once more.

'Brandy and water,' rapidly replied the second voice in the other corner. And then, as if by a concerted movement, a series of bibular invitations and acceptances were rolled backwards and forwards with a volubility of utterance that threw Patter *versus* Clatter into the shade.[14]

'What the Devil can it be?' muttered the Wondersmith, flashing his lantern here and there. 'Ah! it is those Minos.'

So saying, he stopped under one of the wicker cages that hung high up on the wall, and raised the lantern above his head, so as to throw the light upon that particular cage. The hospitable individual who had been extending all these hoarse invitations to partake of intoxicating beverages was an inhabitant of the cage. It was a large mino-bird, who now stood perched on his cross-bar, with his yellowish orange bill sloped slightly over his shoulder, and his white eye cocked knowingly upon the Wondersmith. The respondent voice in the other corner came from another mino-bird, who sat in the dusk in a similar cage, also attentively watching the Wondersmith. These mino-birds, I may remark, in passing, have a singular aptitude for acquiring phrases.

'What'll you take?' repeated the Mino, cocking his other eye upon Herr Hippe.

'*Mon Dieu!* what a bird!' exclaimed the little Frenchman. 'He is, in truth, polite.'

'I don't know what I'll take,' said Hippe, as if replying to the mino-bird; 'but I know what you'll get, old fellow! Filomel, open the cage-doors, and give me the bottle.'

Filomel opened, one after another, the doors of the numberless little cages, thereby arousing from slumber their feathered occupants, who opened their beaks, and stretched their claws, and stared with great surprise at the lantern and the midnight visitors.

By this time the Wondersmith had performed the mysterious manipulations with the bottle, and the manikins were once more in full motion, swarming out of their box, sword and dagger in hand, with their little black eyes glittering fiercely, and their white teeth shining. The little creatures seemed to scent their prey. The gypsies stood in the centre of the shop, watching the proceedings eagerly, while the Lilliputians made in a body towards the wall and commenced climbing from cage to cage. Then was heard a tremendous flittering of wings, and faint, despairing 'quirks' echoed on all sides. In almost every cage there was a fierce manikin thrusting his sword or dagger vigorously into the body of some unhappy bird. It recalled the antique legend of the battles of the Pygmies and the Cranes. The poor love-birds lay with their emerald feathers dabbled in their hearts' blood, shoulder to shoulder in death as in life. Canaries gasped at the bottom of their cages, while the water in their little glass fountains ran red. The bullfinches wore an unnatural crimson on their breasts. The mocking-bird lay on his back, kicking spasmodically, in the last agonies, with a tiny sword-thrust cleaving his melodious throat in twain, so that from the instrument which used to gush with wondrous music only scarlet drops of blood now trickled. The manikins were ruthless. Their faces were ten times wickeder than ever, as they roamed from cage to cage, slaughtering with a fury that seemed entirely unappeasable. Presently the feathery rustlings became fewer and fainter, and the little pipings of despair died away; and in every cage lay a poor murdered minstrel, with the song that abode within him forever quenched;– in every cage but two, and those two were high up on the wall; and in each glared a pair of wild, white eyes; and an orange beak, touch as steel, pointed threateningly down. With the needles which they grasped as swords all wet and warm with blood, and their beadlike eyes flashing in the light of the lantern, the Lilliputian assassins swarmed up the cages in two separate bodies, until they reached the wickets of the habitations in which the Minos abode. Mino saw them coming,– had listened attentively to the many death-struggles of his comrades, and had, in fact, smelt a rat. Accordingly he was ready for the manikins. There he stood at the barbican of his castle, with formidable beak couched like a lance. The manikins made a gallant charge. 'What'll you take?' was rattled out by the Mino, in a deep bass, as with one plunge of his sharp bill he scattered the ranks of the enemy, and sent three of them flying to the floor, where they lay with broken limbs. But the manikins were brave automata, and again they closed and charged the gallant Mino. Again the wicked white eyes of the bird gleamed, and again the orange bill dealt destruction. Everything seemed to be going on swimmingly for Mino, when he found himself attacked in the rear by two treacherous manikins, who had stolen upon him from behind, through the lattice-work of the cage. Quick as lightning the Mino turned to repel this assault, but all too late; two slender quivering threads of steel crossed in his poor body, and he staggered into a corner of the cage. His white eyes closed, then opened; a shiver passed over his body, beginning at his shoulder-tips and dying off in the extreme tips of the wings; he gasped as if for air, and then, with a convulsive shudder, which ruffled all his feathers, croaked out feebly his little speech, 'What'll you take?' Instantly from the opposite corner came the old response, still feebler than the question,– a mere gurgle, as it were, of 'Brandy and water.' Then all was silent. The mino-birds were dead.

'They spill blood like Christians,' said the Wondersmith, gazing fondly on the manikins. 'They will be famous assassins.'

V
TIED UP

Herr Hippe stood in the doorway, scowling. His eyes seemed to scorch the poor hunchback, whose form, physically inferior, crouched before that baneful, blazing glance, while his head, mentally brave, reared itself, as if to redeem the cowardice of the frame to which it belonged. So the attitude of the serpent: the body pliant, yielding, supple; but the crest thrown aloft, erect, and threatening. As for Zonéla, she was frozen in the attitude of motion;– a dancing nymph in coloured marble; agility stunned; elasticity petrified.

Furbelow, astonished at this sudden change, and catching, with all the mysterious rapidity of instinct peculiar to the lower animals, at the enigmatical character of the situation, turned his pleading, melancholy eyes from one to another of the motionless three, as if begging that his humble intellect (pardon me, naturalists, for the use of this word 'intellect' in the matter of a monkey!) should be enlightened as speedily as possible. Not receiving the desired information, he, after the manner of trained animals, returned to his muttons; in other words, he conceived that this unusual entrance, and consequent dramatic *tableau*, meant 'shop'. He therefore dropped Zonéla's hand and pattered on his velvety little feet over towards the grim figure of the Wondersmith, holding out his poor little paw for the customary copper. He had but one idea drilled into him,– soulless creature that he was,– and that was alms. But I have seen creatures that professed to have souls, and that would have been indignant, if you had denied them immortality, who took to the soliciting of alms as naturally as if beggary had been the original sin, and was regularly born with them, and never baptised out of them. I will give these Bandits of the Order of Charity this credit, however, that they knew the best highways and the richest founts of benevolence,– unlike to Furbelow, who, unreasoning and undiscriminating, begged from the first person that was near. Furbelow, owing to this intellectual inferiority to the before-mentioned Alsatians, frequently got more kicks than coppers, and the present supplication which he indulged in towards the Wondersmith was a terrible confirmation of the rule. The reply to the extended pleading paw was what might be called a double-barrelled kick,– a kick to be represented by the power of two when the foot touched the object, multiplied by four when the entire leg formed an angle of forty-five degrees with the spinal column. The long, nervous leg of the Wondersmith caught the little creature in the centre of the body, doubled up his brown, hairy form, till he looked like a fur driving-glove, and sent him whizzing across the room into a far corner, where he dropped senseless and flaccid.

This vengeance which Herr Hippe executed upon Furbelow seemed to have operated as a sort of escape-valve, and he found voice. He hissed out the question, 'Who are you?' to the hunchback; and in listening to that essence of sibillation, it really seemed as if it proceeded from the serpent that curled upon his upper lip.

'Who are you? Deformed dog, who are you? What do you here?'

'My name is Solon,' answered the fearless head of the hunchback, while the frail, cowardly body shivered and trembled inch by inch into a corner.

'So you come to visit my daughter in the night-time, when I am away?' continued the Wondersmith, with a sneering tone that dropped from his snake-wreathed mouth like poison. 'You are a brave and gallant lover, are you not? Where did you win that Order of the Curse of God that decorates your shoulders? The women turn their heads and look after you in the street, when you pass, do they not? lost in admiration of that symmetrical figure, those graceful limbs, that neck pliant as the stem that moors the lotus! Elegant, conquering Christian cripple, what do you here in my daughter's room?'

Can you imagine Jove, limitless in power and wrath, hurling from his vast grasp mountain after mountain upon the struggling Enceladus,– and picture the Titan sinking, sinking, deeper and deeper into the earth, crushed and dying, with nothing visible through the super-incumbent masses of Pelion and Ossa, but a gigantic head and two flaming eyes, that, despite the death which is creeping through each vein, still flash back defiance to the divine enemy?[15] Well, Solon and Herr Hippe presented such a picture, seen through the wrong end of a telescope,– reduced in proportion, but alike in action. Solon's feeble body seemed to sink into utter annihilation beneath the horrible taunts that his enemy hurled at him, while the large, brave brow and unconquered eyes still sent forth a magnetic resistance.

Suddenly the poor hunchback felt his arm grasped. A thrill seemed to run through his entire body. A warm atmosphere, invigorating and full of delicious odour, surrounded him. It appeared as if invisible bandages were twisted all about his limbs, giving him a strange strength. His sinking legs straightened. His powerless arms were braced. Astonished, he glanced round for an instant, and beheld Zonéla, with a world of love burning in her large lambent eyes, wreathing her round white arms about his humped shoulders. Then the poet knew the great sustaining power of love. Solon reared himself boldly.

'Sneer at my poor form,' he cried, in strong vibrating tones, flinging out one long arm and one thin finger at the Wondersmith, as if he would have impaled him like a beetle. 'Humiliate me, if you can. I care not. You are a wretch, and I am honest and pure. This girl is not your daughter. You are like one of those demons in the fairy tales that held beauty and purity locked in infernal spells. I do not fear you, Herr Hippe. There are stories abroad about you in the neighbourhood, and when you pass, people say that they feel evil and blight hovering over their thresholds. You persecute this girl. You are her tyrant. You hate her. I am a cripple. Providence has cast this lump upon my shoulders. But that is nothing. The camel, that is the salvation of the children of the desert, has been given his hump in order that he might bear his human burden better. This girl, who is homeless as the Arab, is my appointed load in life, and, please God, I will carry her on this back, hunched though it may be. I have come to see her, because I love her,– because she loves me. You have no claim on her; so I will take her from you.'

Quick as lightning, the Wondersmith had stridden a few paces, and grasped the poor cripple, who was yet quivering with the departing thunder of his passion. He seized him in his bony, muscular grasp, as he would have seized a puppet, and held him at arm's length gasping and powerless; while Zonéla, pale, breathless, entreating, sank half-kneeling on the floor.

'Your skeleton will be interesting to science when you are dead, Mr. Solon,' hissed the Wondersmith. 'But before I have the pleasure of reducing you to an anatomy, which I will assuredly do, I wish to compliment you on your power of penetration, or sources of information; for I know not if you have derived your knowledge from your own mental research or the efforts of others. You are perfectly correct in your statement, that this charming young person, who day after day parades the streets with a barrel-organ and a monkey,– the last unhappily indisposed at present,– listening to the degrading jokes of ribald boys and depraved men,– you are quite correct, Sir, in stating that she is not my daughter. On the contrary, she is the daughter of a Hungarian nobleman who had the misfortune to incur my displeasure. I had a son, crooked spawn of a Christian!– a son, not like you, cankered, gnarled stump of life that you are,– but a youth tall and fair and noble in aspect, as became a child of one whose lineage makes Pharaoh modern,– a youth whose foot in the dance was as swift and beautiful to look at as the golden sandals of the sun when he dances upon the sea in summer. This youth was virtuous and good; and being of good race, and dwelling in a country where his rank, gypsy as he was, was recognised, he mixed with the proudest of the land. One day he fell in with this accursed Hungarian, a fierce drinker of that Devil's blood called brandy. My child until that hour had avoided this bane of our race. Generous wine he drank, because the soul of the sun our ancestor palpitated in its purple waves. But brandy, which is fallen and accursed wine, as devils are fallen and accursed angels, had never crossed his lips, until in an evil hour he was reduced by this Christian hog, and from that day forth his life was one fiery debauch, which set only in the black waves of death. I vowed vengeance on the destroyer of my child, and I kept my word. I have destroyed *his* child,– not compassed her death, but blighted her life, steeped her in misery and poverty, and now, thanks to the thousand devils, I have discovered a new torture for her heart. She thought to solace her life with a love-episode! Sweet little epicure that she was! She shall have her little crooked lover, shan't she? Oh, yes! She shall have him, cold and stark and livid, with that great, black, heavy hunch, which no back, however broad, can bear, Death, sitting between his shoulders!'

There was something so awful and demoniac in this entire speech and the manner in which it was delivered, that it petrified Zonéla into a mere inanimate figure, whose eyes seemed unalterably fixed on the fierce, cruel face of the Wondersmith. As for Solon, he was paralysed in the grasp of his foe. He heard, but could not reply. His large eyes, dilated with horror to far beyond their ordinary size, expressed unutterable agony.

The last sentence had hardly been hissed out by the gypsy when he took from his pocket a long, thin coil of whipcord, which he entangled in a complicated mesh around the cripple's body. It was not the ordinary binding of a prisoner. The slender lash passed and repassed in a thousand intricate folds over the powerless limbs of the poor humpback. When the operation was completed, he looked as if he had been sewed from head to foot in some singularly ingenious species of network.

'Now, my pretty, lop-sided, little lover,' laughed Herr Hippe, flinging Solon over his shoulder, as a fisherman might fling a net-full of fish, 'we will proceed to put you into your little cage until your little coffin is quite ready. Meanwhile we will lock up your darling beggar-girl to mourn over your untimely end.'

So saying, he stepped from the room with his captive, and securely locked the door behind him.

When he had disappeared, the frozen Zonéla thawed, and with a shriek of anguish flung herself on the inanimate body of Furbelow.

VI

THE POISONING OF THE SWORDS

It was New Year's Eve, and eleven o'clock at night. All over this great land, and in every great city in the land, curly heads were lying on white pillows, dreaming of the coming of the generous Santa Claus. Innumerable stockings hung by countless bedsides. Visions of beautiful toys, passing in splendid pageantry through myriads of dimly lit dormitories, made millions of little hearts palpitate in sleep. Ah! what heavenly toys those were that the children of this soil beheld, that mystic night, in their dreams! Painted cars with orchestral wheels, making music more delicious than the roll of planets. Agile men of cylindrical figure, who sprang unexpectedly out of meek-looking boxes, with a supernatural fierceness in their crimson cheeks and fur-whiskers. Herds of marvellous sheep, with fleeces as impossible as the one that Jason sailed after; animals entirely indifferent to grass and water and 'rot' and 'ticks.' Horses spotted with an astounding regularity, and furnished with the most ingenious methods of locomotion. Slender foreigners, attired in painfully short tunics, whose existence passed in continually turning heels over head down a steep flight of steps, at the bottom of which they lay in an exhausted condition with dislocated limbs, until they were restored to their former elevation, when they went at it again as if nothing had happened. Stately swans, that seemed to have a touch of the ostrich in them; for they swam continually after a piece of iron which was held before them, as if consumed with a ferruginous hunger. Whole farm-yards of roosters, whose tails curled the wrong way,– a slight defect, that was, however, amply atoned for by the size and brilliancy of their scarlet combs, which, it would appear, Providence had intended for pen-wipers. Pears, that, when applied to youthful lips, gave forth sweet and inspiring sounds. Regiments of soldiers, that performed neat, but limited evolutions on cross-jointed contractile battle-fields. All these things, idealised, transfigured, and illuminated by the powers and atmosphere and coloured lamps of Dreamland, did the millions of dear sleeping children behold, the night of the New Year's Eve of which I speak.

It was on this night, when Time was preparing to shed his skin and come out young and golden and glossy as ever,– when, in the vast chambers of the universe, silent and infallible preparations were making for the wonderful birth of the coming year,– when mystic dews were secreted for his baptism, and mystic instruments were tuned in space to welcome him,– it was at this holy and solemn hour that the Wondersmith and his three gypsy companions sat in close conclave in the little parlour before mentioned.

There was a fire roaring in the grate. On a table, nearly in the centre of the room, stood a huge decanter of port wine, that glowed in the blaze which lit the chamber like a flask of crimson fire. On every side, piled in heaps, inanimate, but scowling with the same old wondrous scowl, lay myriads of the manikins, all clutching in their wooden hands their tiny weapons. The Wondersmith held in one hand a small silver bowl filled with a green, glutinous substance, which he was delicately applying, with the aid of a camel's-hair brush, to the tips of tiny swords and daggers. A horrible smile wandered over his sallow face,– a smile as unwholesome in appearance as the sickly light that plays above reeking graveyards.

'Let us drink great draughts, brothers,' he cried, leaving off his strange anointment for a while, to lift a great glass, filled with sparkling liquor, to his lips. 'Let us drink to our approaching triumph. Let us drink to the great poison, Macousha. Subtle seed of Death,– swift hurricane that sweeps away Life,– vast hammer that crushes brain and heart and artery with its resistless weight,– I drink to it.'

'It is a noble decoction, Duke Balthazar,' said the old fortune-teller and mid-wife, Madame Filomel, nodding in her chair as she swallowed her wine in great gulps. 'Where did you obtain it?'

'It is made,' said the Wondersmith, swallowing another great goblet-full of wine ere he replied, 'in the wild woods of Guiana, in silence and in mystery. But one tribe of Indians, the Macoushi Indians, know the secret. It is simmered over fires built of strange woods, and the maker of it dies in the making. The place, for a mile around the spot where it is fabricated, is shunned as accursed. Devils hover over the pot in which it stews; and the birds of the air, scenting the smallest breath of its vapour from far away, drop to earth with paralysed wings, cold and dead.'

'It kills, then, fast?' asked Kerplonne, the artificial eyemaker,– his own eyes gleaming, under the influence of the wine, with a sinister lustre, as if they had been fresh from the factory, and were yet untarnished by use.

'Kills?' echoed the Wondersmith, derisively; 'it is swifter than thunderbolts, stronger than lightning. But you shall see it proved before we let forth our army on the city accursed. You shall see a wretch die, as if smitten by a falling fragment of the sun.'

'What? Do you mean Solon?' asked Oaksmith and the fortune-teller together.

'Ah! you mean the young man who makes the commerce with books?' echoed Kerplonne. 'It is well. His agonies will instruct us.'

'Yes! Solon,' answered Hippe, with a savage accent. 'I hate him, and he shall die this horrid death. Ah! how the little fellows will leap upon him, when I bring him in, bound and helpless, and give their beautiful wicked souls to them! How they will pierce him in ten thousand spots with their poisoned weapons, until his skin turns blue and violet and crimson, and his form swells with the venom,– until his hump is lost in shapeless flesh! He hears what I say, every word of it. He is in the closet next door, and is listening.

73

How comfortable he feels! How the sweat of terror rolls on his brow! How he tries to loosen his bonds, and curses all earth and heaven when he finds that he cannot! Ho! ho! Handsome lover of Zonéla, will she kiss you when you are livid and swollen? Brothers, let us drink again,– drink always. Here, Oaksmith, take these brushes,– and you, Filomel,– and finish the anointing of these swords. This wine is grand. This poison is grand. It is fine to have good wine to drink, and good poison to kill with; is it not?' and, with flushed face and rolling eyes, the Wondersmith continued to drink and use his brush alternately.

The others hastened to follow his example. It was a horrible scene: those four wicked faces; those myriads of tiny faces, just as wicked; the certain unearthly air that pervaded the apartment; the red, unwholesome glare cast by the fire; the wild and reckless way in which the weird company drank the red-illumined wine.

The anointing of the swords went on rapidly, and the wine went as rapidly down the throats of the four poisoners. Their faces grew more and more inflamed each instant; their eyes shone like rolling fireballs; their hair was moist and dishevelled. The old fortune-teller rocked to and fro in her chair, like those legless plaster figures that sway upon convex loaded bottoms. All four began to mutter incoherent sentences, and babble unintelligible wickednesses. Still the anointing of the swords went on.

'I see the faces of millions of young corpses,' babbled Herr Hippe, gazing, with swimming eyes, into the silver bowl that contained the Macousha poison,– 'all young, all Christians,– and the little fellows dancing, dancing, and stabbing, stabbing. Filomel, Filomel, I say!'

'Well, Grand Duke,' snored the old woman, giving a violent lurch.

'Where's the bottle of souls?'

'In my right-hand pocket, Herr Hippe'; and she felt, so as to assure herself that it was there. She half drew out the black bottle, before described in this narrative, and let it slide again into her pocket,– let it slide again, but it did not completely regain its former place. Caught by some accident, it hung half out, swaying over the edge of the pocket, as the fat midwife rolled backwards and forwards in her drunken efforts at equilibrium.

'All right,' said Herr Hippe, 'perfectly right! Let's drink.'

He reached out his hand for his glass, and, with a dull sigh, dropped on the table, in the instantaneous slumber of intoxication. Oaksmith soon fell back in his chair, breathing heavily. Kerplonne followed. And the heavy, stertorous breathing of Filomel told that she slumbered also; but still her chair retained its rocking motion, and still the bottle of souls balanced itself on the edge of her pocket.

VII
LET LOOSE

Sure enough, Solon heard every word of the fiendish talk of the Wondersmith. For how many days he had been shut up, bound in the terrible net, in that dark closet, he did not know; but now he felt that his last hour was come. His little strength was completely worn out in efforts to disentangle himself. Once a day a door opened, and Herr Hippe placed a crust of bread and a cup of water within his reach. On this meagre fare he had subsisted. It was a hard life; but, bad as it was, it was better than the horrible death that menaced him. His brain reeled with terror at the prospect of it. Then, where was

Zonéla? Why did she not come to his rescue? But she was, perhaps, dead. The darkness, too, appalled him. A faint light, when the moon was bright, came at night through a chink far up in the wall; and the only other hole in the chamber was an aperture through which, at some former time, a stove-pipe had been passed. Even if he were free, there would have been small hope of escape; but, laced as it were in a network of steel, what was to be done? He groaned and writhed upon the floor, and tore at the boards with his hands, which were free from the wrists down. All else was as solidly laced up as an Indian papoose.[16] Nothing but pride kept him from shrieking aloud, when, on the night of New Year's Eve, he heard the fiendish Hippe recite the programme of his murder.

While he was thus wailing and gnashing his teeth in darkness and torture, he heard a faint noise above his head. Then something seemed to leap from the ceiling and alight softly on the floor. He shuddered with terror. Was it some new torture of the Wondersmith's invention? The next moment, he felt some small animal crawling over his body, and a soft, silky paw was pushed timidly across his face. His heart leaped with joy.

'It is Furbelow!' he cried. 'Zonéla has sent him. He came through the stove-pipe hole.'

It was Furbelow, indeed, restored to life by Zonéla's care, and who had come down a narrow tube, that no human being could have threaded, to console the poor captive. The monkey nestled closely into the hunchback's bosom, and, as he did so, Solon felt something cold and hard hanging from his neck. He touched it. It was sharp. By the dim light that struggled through the aperture high up in the wall, he discovered a knife, suspended by a bit of cord. Ah! how the blood came rushing through the veins that crossed over and through his heart, when life and liberty came to him in this bit of rusty steel! With his manacled hands he loosened the heaven-sent weapon; a few cuts were rapidly made in the cunning network of cord that enveloped his limbs, and in a few seconds he was free! – cramped and faint with hunger, but free! – free to move, to use the limbs that God had given him for his preservation,– free to fight,– to die fighting, perhaps,– but still to die free. He ran to the door. The bolt was a weak one, for the Wondersmith had calculated more surely on his prison of cords than on any jail of stone,– and more; and with a few efforts the door opened. He went cautiously out into the darkness, with Furbelow perched on his shoulder, pressing his cold muzzle against his cheek. He had made but a few steps when a trembling hand was put into his, and in another moment Zonéla's palpitating heart was pressed against his own. One long kiss, an embrace, a few whispered words, and the hunchback and the girl stole softly towards the door of the chamber in which the four gypsies slept. All seemed still; nothing but the hard breathing of the sleepers, and the monotonous rocking of Madame Filomel's chair broke the silence. Solon stooped down and put his eye to the keyhole, through which a red bar of light streamed into the entry. As he did so, his foot crushed some brittle substance that lay just outside the door; at the same moment a howl of agony was heard to issue from the room within. Solon started; nor did he know that at that instant he had crushed into dust Monsieur Kerplonne's supernumerary eye, and the owner, though wrapt in a drunken sleep, felt the pang quiver through his brain.

While Solon peeped through the keyhole, all in the room was motionless. He had not gazed, however, for many seconds, when the chair of the fortune-teller gave a sudden lurch, and the black bottle, already hanging half out of her wide pocket, slipped entirely from its resting-place, and, falling heavily to the ground, shivered into fragments.

Then took place an astonishing spectacle. The myriads of armed dolls, that lay in piles about the room, became suddenly imbued with motion. They stood up straight, their tiny limbs moved, their black eyes flashed with wicked purposes, their thread-like swords gleamed as they waved them to and fro. The villainous souls imprisoned in the bottle began to work within them. Like the Lilliputians, when they found the giant Gulliver asleep, they scaled in swarms the burly sides of the four sleeping gypsies. At every step they took, they drove their thin swords and quivering daggers into the flesh of the drunken authors of their being. To stab and kill was their mission, and they stabbed and killed with incredible fury. They clustered on the Wondersmith's sallow cheeks and sinewy throat, piercing every portion with their diminutive poisoned blades. Filomel's fat carcass was alive with them. They blackened the spare body of Monsieur Kerplonne. They covered Oaksmith's huge form like a cluster of insects.

Overcome completely with the fumes of wine, these tiny wounds did not for a few moments awaken the sleeping victims. But the swift and deadly poison Macousha, with which the weapons had been so fiendishly anointed, began to work. Herr Hippe, stung into sudden life, leaped to his feet, with a dwarf army clinging to his clothes and his hands,– always stabbing, stabbing, stabbing. For an instant, a look of stupid bewilderment clouded his face; then the horrible truth burst upon him. He gave a shriek like that which a horse utters when he finds himself fettered and surrounded by fire,– a shriek that curdled the air for miles and miles.

'Oaksmith! Kerplonne! Filomel! Awake! awake! We are lost! The souls have got loose! We are dead! poisoned! Oh, accursed ones! Oh, demons, ye are slaying me! Ah! fiends of Hell!'

Aroused by these frightful howls, the three gypsies sprang also to their feet, to find themselves stung to death by the manikins. They raved, they shrieked, they swore. They staggered round the chamber. Blinded in the eyes by the ever-stabbing weapons,– with the poison already burning in their veins like red-hot lead,– their forms swelling and discolouring visibly every moment,– their howls and attitudes and furious gestures made the scene look like a chamber in Hell.

Maddened beyond endurance, the Wondersmith, half-blind and choking with the venom that had congested all the blood-vessels of his body, seized dozens of the manikins and dashed them into the fire, trampling them down with his feet.

'Ye shall die too, if I die,' he cried, with a roar like that of a tiger. 'Ye shall burn, if I burn. I gave ye life,– I give ye death. Down! – down! – burn! – flame! Fiends that ye are, to slay us! Help me, brothers! Before we die, let us have our revenge!'

On this, the other gypsies, themselves maddened by approaching death, began hurling manikins, by handfuls, into the fire. The little creatures, being wooden of body, quickly caught the flames, and an awful struggle for life took place in miniature in the grate. Some of them escaped from between the bars and ran about the room, blazing, writhing in agony, and igniting the curtains and other draperies that hung around. Others fought and stabbed one another in the very core of the fire, like combating salamanders. Meantime, the motions of the gypsies grew more languid and slow, and their curses were uttered in choked guttural tones. The faces of all four were spotted with red and green and violet, like so many eggplants. Their bodies were swollen to a frightful size, and at last they dropped on the floor, like overripe fruit shaken from the boughs by the winds of autumn.

The chamber was now a sheet of fire. The flames roared round and round, as if seeking for escape, licking every projecting cornice and sill with greedy tongues, as the serpent licks his prey before he swallows it. A hot, putrid breath came through the keyhole and smote Solon and Zonéla like a wind of death. They clasped each other's hands with a moan of terror, and fled from the house.

The next morning, when the young year was just unclosing its eyes, and the happy children all over the great city were peeping from their beds into the myriads of stockings hanging near by, the blue skies of heaven shone through a black network of stone and charred rafters. These were all that remained of the habitation of Herr Hippe, the Wondersmith.

What Was It?
A Mystery

It is, I confess, with considerable diffidence that I approach the strange narrative which I am about to relate. The events which I purpose detailing are of so extraordinary and unheard-of a character that I am quite prepared to meet with an unusual amount of incredulity and scorn. I accept all such beforehand. I have, I trust, the literary courage to face unbelief. I have, after mature consideration, resolved to narrate, in as simple and straightforward a manner as I can compass, some facts that passed under my observation in the month of July last, and which, in the annals of the mysteries of physical science, are wholly unparalleled.

I live at No. — Twenty-sixth Street, in this city. The house is in some respects a curious one. It has enjoyed for the last two years the reputation of being haunted. It is a large and stately residence, surrounded by what was once a garden, but which is now only a green enclosure used for bleaching clothes. The dry basin of what has been a fountain, and a few fruit-trees, ragged and unpruned, indicate that this spot, in past days, was a pleasant, shady retreat, filled with fruits and flowers and the sweet murmur of waters.

The house is very spacious. A hall of noble size leads to a vast spiral staircase winding through its centre, while the various apartments are of imposing dimensions. It was built some fifteen or twenty years since by Mr. A——, the well-known New York merchant, who five years ago threw the commercial world into convulsions by a stupendous bank fraud. Mr. A——, as everyone knows, escaped to Europe, and died not long after of a broken heart. Almost immediately after the news of his decease reached this country, and was verified, the report spread in Twenty-sixth Street that No.— was haunted. Legal measures had dispossessed the widow of its former owner, and it was inhabited merely by a caretaker and his wife, placed there by the house agent into whose hands it had passed for purposes of renting or sale. These people declared that they were troubled with unnatural noises. Doors were opened without any visible agency. The remnants of furniture scattered through the various rooms were, during the night, piled one upon the other by unknown hands. Invisible feet passed up and down the stairs in broad daylight, accompanied by the rustle of unseen silk dresses, and the gliding of viewless hands along the massive balusters. The caretaker and his wife declared that they would live there no longer. The house agent laughed, dismissed them, and put others in their place. The noises and supernatural manifestations continued. The neighbourhood caught up the story, and the house remained untenanted for three years. Several persons negotiated for it; but somehow, always before the bargain was closed, they heard the unpleasant rumours, and declined to treat any further.

It was in this state of things that my landlady – who at that time kept a boarding-house in Bleecker Street, and who wished to move farther up town – conceived the bold idea of renting No.— Twenty-sixth Street. Happening to have in her house rather a plucky and philosophical set of boarders, she laid down her scheme before us, stating candidly everything she had heard respecting the ghostly qualities of the establishment to which she wished to remove us. With the exception of two timid persons,– a sea captain and a returned Californian, who immediately gave notice that they would leave,– all of Mrs. Moffat's guests declared that they would accompany her in her chivalric incursion into the abode of spirits.

Our removal was effected in the month of May, and we were all charmed with our new residence. The portion of Twenty-sixth Street where our house is situated – between Seventh and Eighth Avenues – is one of the pleasantest localities in New York. The gardens back of the houses, running down nearly to the Hudson, form, in the summer time, a perfect avenue of verdure. The air is pure and invigorating, sweeping, as it does, straight across the river from the Weehawken heights, and even the ragged garden which surrounded the house on two sides, although displaying on washing days rather too much clothesline, still gave us a piece of greensward to look at, and a cool retreat in the summer evenings, where we smoked our cigars in the dusk, and watched the fireflies flashing their dark-lanterns in the long grass.

Of course we had no sooner established ourselves at No.— than we began to expect the ghosts. We absolutely awaited their advent with eagerness. Our dinner conversation was supernatural. One of the boarders, who had purchased Mrs. Crowe's 'Night Side of Nature' for his own private delectation, was regarded as a public enemy by the entire household for not having bought twenty copies. The man led a life of supreme wretchedness while he was reading this volume. A system of espionage was established, of which he was the victim. If he incautiously laid the book down for an instant and left the room, it was immediately seized and read aloud in secret places to a select few. I found myself a person of immense importance, it having leaked out that I was tolerably well versed in the history of supernaturalism, and had once written a story, entitled 'The Pot of Tulips,' for *Harper's Monthly*, the foundation of which was a ghost.[17] If a table or a wainscot panel happened to warp when we were assembled in the large drawing-room, there was an instant silence, and everyone was prepared for an immediate clanking of chains and a spectral form.

After a month of psychological excitement, it was with the utmost dissatisfaction that we were forced to acknowledge that nothing in the remotest degree approaching the supernatural had manifested itself. Once the black butler asseverated that his candle had been blown out by some invisible agency while he was undressing himself for the night; but as I had more than once discovered this coloured gentleman in a condition when one candle must have appeared to him like two, I thought it possible that, by going a step farther in his potations, he might have reversed his phenomenon, and seen no candle at all where he ought to have beheld one.

Things were in this state when an incident took place so awful and inexplicable in its character that my reason fairly reels at the bare memory of the occurrence. It was the 10th of July. After dinner was over I repaired with my friend, Dr. Hammond, to the garden to smoke my evening pipe. Independent of certain mental sympathies which existed between the Doctor and myself, we were linked together by a vice. We both smoked opium. We knew each other's secret, and respected it. We enjoyed together that wonderful expansion of thought, that marvellous intensifying of the perceptive faculties, that boundless feeling of existence when we seem to have points of contact with the whole universe,– in short, that unimaginable spiritual bliss, which I would not surrender for a throne, and which I hope you, reader, will never, never taste.

Those hours of opium happiness which the Doctor and I spent together in secret were regulated with a scientific accuracy. We did not blindly smoke the drug of paradise, and leave our dreams to chance. While smoking, we carefully steered our conversation through the brightest and calmest channels of thought. We talked of the East, and endeavoured to recall the magical panorama of its glowing scenery. We criticised the most sensuous poets,– those who painted life ruddy with health, brimming with passion, happy in the possession of youth and strength and beauty. If we talked of Shakespeare's 'The Tempest',[18] we lingered over Ariel, and avoided Caliban. Like the Guebers, we turned our faces to the East, and saw only the sunny side of the world.[19]

This skilful colouring of our train of thought produced in our subsequent visions a corresponding tone. The splendours of Arabian fairyland dyed our dreams. We paced the narrow strip of grass with the tread and port of kings. The song of the *Rana arborea*, while he clung to the bark of the ragged plum-tree, sounded like the strains of divine musicians.[20] Houses, walls, and streets melted like rain clouds, and vistas of unimaginable glory stretched away before us. It was a rapturous companionship. We enjoyed the vast delight more perfectly because, even in our most ecstatic moments, we were conscious of each other's presence. Our pleasures, while individual, were still twin, vibrating and moving in musical accord.

On the evening in question, the 10th of July, the Doctor and myself found ourselves in an unusually metaphysical mood. We lit our large meerschaums, filled with fine Turkish tobacco, in the core of which burned a little black nut of opium, that, like the nut in the fairy tale, held within its narrow limits wonders beyond the reach of kings; we paced to and fro, conversing. A strange perversity dominated the currents of our thought. They would *not* flow through the sun-lit channels into which we strove to divert them. For some unaccountable reason they constantly diverged into dark and lonesome beds, where a continual gloom brooded. It was in vain that, after our old fashion, we flung ourselves on the shores of the East, and talked of its gay bazaars, of the splendours of the time of

Haroun, of harems and golden palaces. Black afreets continually arose from the depths of our talk, and expanded, like the one the fisherman released from the copper vessel, until they blotted everything bright from our vision. Insensibly, we yielded to the occult force that swayed us, and indulged in gloomy speculation. We had talked some time upon the proneness of the human mind to mysticism, and the almost universal love of the Terrible, when Hammond suddenly said to me:

'What do you consider to be the greatest element of Terror?'

The question, I own, puzzled me. That many things were terrible, I knew. Stumbling over a corpse in the dark; beholding, as I once did, a woman floating down a deep and rapid river, with wildly-lifted arms, and awful, upturned face, uttering, as she sank, shrieks that rent one's heart, while we, the spectators, stood frozen at a window which overhung the river at a height of sixty feet, unable to make the slightest effort to save her, but dumbly watching her last supreme agony and her disappearance. A shattered wreck, with no life visible, encountered floating listlessly on the ocean, is a terrible object, for it suggests a huge terror, the proportions of which are veiled. But it now struck me for the first time that there must be one great and ruling embodiment of fear, a King of Terrors to which all others must succumb. What might it be? To what train of circumstances would it owe its existence?

'I confess, Hammond,' I replied to my friend, 'I never considered the subject before. That there must be one Something more terrible than any other thing, I feel. I cannot attempt, however, even the most vague definition.'

'I am somewhat like you, Harry,' he answered. 'I feel my capacity to experience a terror greater than anything yet conceived by the human mind. Something combining in fearful and unnatural amalgamation hitherto supposed incompatible elements. The calling of the voices in Brockden Brown's novel of 'Wieland' is awful; so is the picture of the Dweller of the Threshold in Bulwer's 'Zanoni'; 'but,' he added, shaking his head gloomily, 'there is something more horrible still than these.'

'Look here, Hammond,' I rejoined, 'let us drop this kind of talk, for Heaven's sake. We shall suffer for it, depend on it.'

'I don't know what's the matter with me tonight,' he replied, 'but my brain is running upon all sorts of weird and awful thoughts. I feel as if I could write a story like Hoffman tonight, if I were only master of a literary style.'[21]

'Well, if we are going to be Hoffmannesque in our talk, I'm off to bed. Opium and nightmares should never be brought together. How sultry it is! Good night, Hammond.'

'Good night, Harry. Pleasant dreams to you.'

'To you, gloomy wretch, afreets, ghouls, and enchanters.'

We parted, and each sought his respective chamber. I undressed quickly and got into bed, taking with me, according to my usual custom, a book, over which I generally read myself to sleep. I opened the volume as soon as I had laid my head upon the pillow, and instantly flung it to the other side of the room. It was Goudon's 'History of Monsters' – a curious French work, which I had lately imported from Paris, but which, in the state of mind I was then in, was anything but an agreeable companion. I resolved to go to sleep at once; so, turning down my gas until nothing but a little blue point of light glimmered on the top of the tube, I composed myself to rest.

The room was in total darkness. The atom of gas that still remained lighted did not illuminate a distance of three inches round the burner. I desperately drew my arm across my eyes, as if to shut out even the darkness, and tried to think of nothing. It was in vain. The confounded themes touched on by Hammond in the garden kept obtruding themselves on my brain. I battled against them. I erected ramparts of would-be blankness of intellect to keep them out. They still crowded upon me. While I was lying still as a corpse, hoping that by a perfect physical inaction I should hasten mental repose, an awful incident occurred. A Something dropped, as it seemed, from the ceiling, plumb upon my chest, and the next instant I felt two bony hands encircling my throat, endeavouring to choke me.

I am no coward, and am possessed of considerable physical strength. The suddenness of the attack, instead of stunning me, strung every nerve to its highest tension. My body acted from instinct, before my brain had time to realise the terrors of my position. In an instant I wound two muscular arms around the creature, and squeezed it, with all the strength of despair, against my chest. In a few seconds the bony hands that had fastened on my throat loosened their hold, and I was free to breathe once more. Then commenced a struggle of awful intensity. Immersed in the most profound darkness, totally ignorant of the nature of the Thing by which I was so suddenly attacked, finding my grasp slipping every moment, by reason, it seemed to me, of the entire nakedness of my assailant, bitten with sharp teeth in the shoulder, neck, and chest, having every moment to protect my throat against a pair of sinewy, agile hands, which my utmost efforts could not confine – these were a combination of circumstances to combat which required all the strength and skill and courage that I possessed.

At last, after a silent, deadly, exhausting struggle, I got my assailant under by a series of incredible efforts of strength.

Once pinned, with my knee on what I made out to be its chest, I knew that I was victor. I rested for a moment to breathe. I heard the creature beneath me panting in the darkness, and felt the violent throbbing of a heart. It was apparently as exhausted as I was; that was one comfort. At this moment I remembered that I usually placed under my pillow, before going to bed, a large yellow silk pocket handkerchief, for use during the night. I felt for it instantly; it was there. In a few seconds more I had, after a fashion, pinioned the creature's arms.

I now felt tolerably secure. There was nothing more to be done but to turn on the gas, and, having first seen what my midnight assailant was like, arouse the household. I will confess to being actuated by a certain pride in not giving the alarm before; I wished to make the capture alone and unaided.

Never losing my hold for an instant, I slipped from the bed to the floor, dragging my captive with me. I had but a few steps to make to reach the gas-burner; these I made with the greatest caution, holding the creature in a grip like a vice. At last I got within arm's-length of the tiny speck of blue light which told me where the gas-burner lay. Quick as lightning I released my grasp with one hand and let on the full flood of light. Then I turned to look at my captive.

I cannot even attempt to give any definition of my sensations the instant after I turned on the gas. I suppose I must have shrieked with terror, for in less than a minute afterward my room was crowded with the inmates of the house. I shudder now as I think of that awful moment. *I saw nothing!* Yes; I had one arm firmly clasped round a breathing, panting, corporeal shape, my other hand gripped with all its strength a throat as warm, and apparently fleshly, as my own; and yet, with this living substance in my grasp, with its body pressed against my own, and all in the bright glare of a large jet of gas, I absolutely beheld nothing! Not even an outline,– a vapour!

I do not, even at this hour, realise the situation in which I found myself. I cannot recall the astounding incident thoroughly. Imagination in vain tries to compass the awful paradox.

It breathed. I felt its warm breath upon my cheek. It struggled fiercely. It had hands. They clutched me. Its skin was smooth, just like my own. There it lay, pressed close up against me, solid as stone,– and yet utterly invisible!

I wonder that I did not faint or go mad on the instant. Some wonderful instinct must have sustained me; for, absolutely, in place of loosening my hold on the terrible Enigma, I seemed to gain an additional strength in my moment of horror, and tightened my grasp with such wonderful force that I felt the creature shivering with agony.

Just then Hammond entered my room at the head of the household. As soon as he beheld my face – which, I suppose, must have been an awful sight to look at – he hastened forward, crying,

'Great heaven, Harry! what has happened?'

'Hammond! Hammond!' I cried, 'come here. Oh! this is awful! I have been attacked in bed by something or other, which I have hold of; but I can't see it – I can't see it!'

Hammond, doubtless struck by the unfeigned horror expressed in my countenance, made one or two steps forward with an anxious yet puzzled expression. A very audible titter burst from the remainder of my visitors. This suppressed laughter made me furious. To laugh at a human being in my position! It was the worst species of cruelty. *Now*, I can understand why the appearance of a man struggling violently, as it would seem, with an airy nothing, and calling for assistance against a vision, should have appeared ludicrous. *Then*, so great was my rage against the mocking crowd that had I the power I would have stricken them dead where they stood.

'Hammond! Hammond!' I cried again, despairingly, 'for God's sake come to me. I can hold the – the Thing but a short while longer. It is overpowering me. Help me! Help me!'

'Harry,' whispered Hammond, approaching me, 'you have been smoking too much opium.'

'I swear to you, Hammond, that this is no vision,' I answered, in the same low tone. 'Don't you see how it shakes my whole frame with its struggles? If you don't believe me, convince yourself. Feel it,– touch it.'

Hammond advanced and laid his hand on the spot I indicated. A wild cry of horror burst from him. He had felt it!

In a moment he had discovered somewhere in my room a long piece of cord, and was the next instant winding it and knotting it about the body of the unseen being that I clasped in my arms.

'Harry,' he said, in a hoarse, agitated voice, for, though he preserved his presence of mind, he was deeply moved, 'Harry, it's all safe now. You may let go, old fellow, if you're tired. The Thing can't move.'

I was utterly exhausted, and I gladly loosed my hold.

Hammond stood holding the ends of the cord that bound the Invisible, twisted round his hand, while before him, self-supporting as it were, he beheld a rope laced and interlaced, and stretching tightly round a vacant space. I never saw a man look so thoroughly stricken with awe. Nevertheless his face expressed all the courage and determination which I knew him to possess. His lips, although white, were set firmly, and one could perceive at a glance that, although stricken with fear, he was not daunted.

The confusion that ensued among the guests of the house who were witnesses of this extraordinary scene between Hammond and myself,– who beheld the pantomime of binding this struggling Something,– who beheld me almost sinking from physical exhaustion when my task of jailer was over – the confusion and terror that took possession of the bystanders, when they saw all this, was beyond description. Many of the weaker ones fled from the apartment. The few who remained clustered near the door, and could not be induced to approach Hammond and his Charge. Still incredulity broke out through their terror. They had not the courage to satisfy themselves, and yet they doubted. It was in vain that I begged of some of the men to come near and convince themselves by touch of the existence of a living being in that room which was invisible. They were incredulous, but did not dare to undeceive themselves. How could a solid, living, breathing body be invisible? they asked. My reply was this. I gave a sign to Hammond, and both of us – conquering our fearful repugnance to touch the invisible creature – lifted it from the ground, manacled as it was, and took it to my bed. Its weight was about that of a boy of fourteen.

'Now, my friends,' I said, as Hammond and myself held the creature suspended over the bed, 'I can give you self-evident proof that here is a solid, ponderable body which, nevertheless, you cannot see. Be good enough to watch the surface of the bed attentively.'

I was astonished at my own courage in treating this strange event so calmly; but I had recovered from my first terror, and felt a sort of scientific pride in the affair which dominated every other feeling.

The eyes of the bystanders were immediately fixed on my bed. At a given signal Hammond and I let the creature fall. There was the dull sound of a heavy body alighting on a soft mass. The timbers of the bed creaked. A deep impression marked itself distinctly on the pillow, and on the bed itself. The crowd who witnessed this gave a sort of low, universal cry, and rushed from the room. Hammond and I were left alone with our Mystery.

We remained silent for some time, listening to the low, irregular breathing of the creature on the bed, and watching the rustle of the bedclothes as it impotently struggled to free itself from confinement. Then Hammond spoke.

'Harry, this is awful.'

'Ay, awful.'

'But not unaccountable.'

'Not unaccountable! What do you mean? Such a thing has never occurred since the birth of the world. I know not what to think, Hammond. God grant that I am not mad, and that this is not an insane fantasy!'

'Let us reason a little, Harry. Here is a solid body which we touch, but which we cannot see. The fact is so unusual that it strikes us with terror. Is there no parallel, though, for such a phenomenon? Take a piece of pure glass. It is tangible and transparent. A certain chemical coarseness is all that prevents its being so entirely transparent as to be totally invisible. It is not *theoretically impossible,* mind you, to make a glass which shall not reflect a single ray of light – a glass so pure and homogeneous in its atoms that the rays from the sun shall pass through it as they do through the air, refracted but not reflected. We do not see the air, and yet we feel it.'

'That's all very well, Hammond, but these are inanimate substances. Glass does not breathe, air does not breathe. *This* thing has a heart that palpitates. A will that moves it. Lungs that play, and inspire and respire.'

'You forget the strange phenomena of which we have so often heard of late,' answered the Doctor, gravely. 'At the meetings called 'spirit circles,' invisible hands have been thrust into the hands of those persons round the table – warm, fleshly hands that seemed to pulsate with mortal life.'

'What? Do you think, then, that this thing is–'

'I don't know what it is,' was the solemn reply; 'but please the gods I will, with your assistance, thoroughly investigate it.'

We watched together, smoking many pipes, all night long, by the bedside of the unearthly being that tossed and panted until it was apparently wearied out. Then we learned by the low, regular breathing that it slept.

The next morning the house was all astir. The boarders congregated on the landing outside my room, and Hammond and myself were lions. We had to answer a thousand questions as to the state of our extraordinary prisoner, for as yet not one person in the house except ourselves could be induced to set foot in the apartment.

The creature was awake. This was evidenced by the convulsive manner in which the bedclothes were moved in its efforts to escape. There was something truly terrible in beholding, as it were, those second-hand indications of the terrible writhings and agonised struggles for liberty which themselves were invisible.

Hammond and myself had racked our brains during the long night to discover some means by which we might realise the shape and general appearance of the Enigma. As well as we could make out by passing our hands over the creature's form, its outlines and lineaments were human. There was a mouth; a round, smooth head without hair; a nose, which, however, was little elevated above the cheeks; and its hands and feet felt like those of a boy. At first we thought of placing the being on a smooth surface and tracing its outline with chalk, as shoemakers trace the outline of the foot. This plan was given up as being of no value. Such an outline would give not the slightest idea of its conformation.

A happy thought struck me. We would take a cast of it in plaster of Paris. This would give us the solid figure, and satisfy all our wishes. But how to do it? The movements of the creature would disturb the setting of the plastic covering, and distort the mould. Another thought. Why not give it chloroform? It had respiratory organs – that was evident by its breathing. Once reduced to a state of insensibility, we could do with it what we would. Doctor X—— was sent for; and after the worthy physician had recovered from the first shock of amazement, he proceeded to administer the chloroform. In three minutes afterward we were enabled to remove the fetters from the creature's body, and a well-known modeller of this city was busily engaged in covering the invisible form with the moist clay. In five minutes more we had a mould, and before evening a rough *fac-simile* of the Mystery. It was shaped like a man. Distorted, uncouth, and horrible, but still a man. It was small, not over four feet and some inches in height, and its limbs betrayed a muscular development that was unparalleled. Its face surpassed in hideousness anything I had ever seen. Gustave Doré, or Callot, or Tony Johannot, never conceived anything so horrible.[22] There is a face in one of the latter's illustrations to *Un Voyage où il vous plaira*, which somewhat approaches the countenance of this creature, but does not equal it. It was the physiognomy of what I should have fancied a ghoul to be. It looked as if it was capable of feeding on human flesh.

Having satisfied our curiosity, and bound everyone in the house to secrecy, it became a question what was to be done with our Enigma? It was impossible that we should keep such a horror in our house; it was equally impossible that such an awful being should be let loose upon the world. I confess that I would have gladly voted for the creature's destruction. But who would shoulder the responsibility? Who would undertake the execution of this horrible semblance of a human being? Day after day this question was deliberated gravely. The boarders all left the house. Mrs. Moffat was in despair, and threatened Hammond and myself with all sorts of legal penalties if we did not remove the Horror. Our answer was, 'We will go if you like, but we decline taking this creature with us. Remove it yourself if you please. It appeared in your house. On you the responsibility rests.' To this there was, of course, no answer. Mrs. Moffat could not obtain for love or money a person who would even approach the Mystery.

The most singular part of the transaction was that we were entirely ignorant of what the creature habitually fed on. Everything in the way of nutriment that we could think of was placed before it, but was never touched. It was awful to stand by, day after day, and see the clothes toss, and hear the hard breathing, and know that it was starving.

Ten, twelve days, a fortnight passed, and it still lived. The pulsations of the heart, however, were daily growing fainter, and had now nearly ceased altogether. It was evident that the creature was dying for want of sustenance. While this terrible life struggle was going on, I felt miserable. I could not sleep of nights. Horrible as the creature was, it was pitiful to think of the pangs it was suffering.

At last it died. Hammond and I found it cold and stiff one morning in the bed. The heart had ceased to beat, the lungs to inspire. We hastened to bury it in the garden. It was a strange funeral, the dropping of that viewless corpse into the damp hole. The cast of its form I gave to Dr. X——, who keeps it in his museum in Tenth Street.

As I am on the eve of a long journey from which I may not return, I have drawn up this narrative of an event the most singular that has ever come to my knowledge.

Harry Escott

[NOTE. It was rumoured that the proprietors of a well-known museum in this city had made arrangements with Dr. X—— to exhibit to the public the singular cast which Mr. Escott deposited with him. So extraordinary a history cannot fail to attract universal attention.]

NOTES

1. A bull's eye was a particular type of lens with a series of concentric rings which was used to focus light in lanterns and lighthouses.

2. These are all famous scientists and miscroscopists. Anton Van Leeuewenhoek (1632–1723), whom O'Brien draws on in particular in this tale, has been dubbed the father of microbiology for the many advances he made in designing the microscope.

3. Francis Herbert Wenham (1824–1908) was another prominent microscopist.

4. Argus was a giant in Greek mythology with many eyes.

5. The Upper Ten, or Upper Ten Thousand, was a phrase coined by Nathaniel Parker Willis in 1852 to describe the upper class of New York.

6. A Carcel lamp was an oil lamp in common use in France in the nineteenth century.

7. A Malay creese is a Sumatran knife.

8. Calcination is a thermal process that can cause loss of moisture or oxidation, effectively ruining a lens.

9. The multitude of quotes attributed to Alexander the Great makes it difficult to determine precisely which one O'Brien is thinking of here, but the most likely is this one in relation to other worlds: 'Do you not think it a matter worthy of lamentation that when there is such a vast multitude of them, we have not yet conquered one?'

10. In Greek mythology Salmacis tried unsuccessfully to seduce the handsome Hermaphroditus, eventually resorting to physical force and divine intervention to ensnare him.

11. *The Count de Gabalis* is an anonymously written text from the seventeenth century used by the Rosicrucians (a Christian sect), which covers five discourses on man and nature.

12. 'Duke of Egypt' was one of many grand titles used by gypsies for their leaders.

13. A region in Latvia.

14. 'Patter *versus* Clatter' was a farce by Charles James Matthews (1803–78), a British actor who toured America on three occasions, and was famous for delivering his speeches at rapid speed.

15. In Greek mythology Enceladus was a giant who battled, unsuccessfully, with the Olympic gods.

16. A papoose is a term used both to describe Native American children and the cradle boards in which they were secured to be carried on their mothers' backs, the design of which had the child completely secured except for their head.

17. One of many examples in O'Brien's work of autobiography spilling into fiction: 'The Pot of Tulips' was one of his earlier stories, also narrated by the character of Harry Escott, and published in *Harper's Monthly* in 1855.

18. In the original text, O'Brien mistakenly writes 'A Midsummer Night's Dream', though Ariel and Caliban actually appear in *The Tempest*.

19. The Guebers were one of the many religious faiths in Asia of whom American missionaries sent back reports; a common feature of a lot of these groups was a strong reverence for the sun.

20. The *Rana arborea* is a tree frog.

21. E.T.A. Hoffmann was a celebrated writer of gothic fiction.

22. Gustave Doré illustrated, among other things, *Paradise Lost*, Jacques Callot was a seventeenth century engraver most famous for a series of prints called *Les Grandes Miseres de la Guerre* depicting the horrors of war, while Tony Johannot's work for *Voyage où il vous plaira* ('A journey to where you please') verged on the surreal and grotesque.

BIOGRAPHICAL NOTE

Fitz-James O'Brien was born Michael O'Brien in County Cork, Ireland, in 1828. Alleged to have been educated at Trinity College, Dublin, he spent two years (and most of a large inheritance) in London before moving to the United States in 1852. Here he began contributing articles to a number of newspapers and periodicals, including *The New York Times*, *Vanity Fair*, *Putnam's* and *Harper's*. When the American Civil War broke out in 1861 he joined the New York National Guard and was wounded in February the following year. He did not recover, and died in Cumberland, Maryland, in April 1862.

Pete Orford gained his PhD from the Shakespeare Institute for researching the modern reception of Shakespeare's history plays. Since then he has become embroiled in an academic *ménage à trois* with Shakespeare and Dickens, presenting papers at conferences on both writers, as well as publishing articles and books. He is the general editor of *Divining Thoughts: Future Directions in Shakespeare Studies* and has edited three collections of Dickens' writings for Hesperus Press, *On Travel* (2009), *On London* (2010) and *On Theatre* (2011). He is currently researching the life and works of Fitz-James O'Brien.

SELECTED TITLES FROM HESPERUS PRESS

Author	Title	Foreword writer
Pietro Aretino	*The School of Whoredom*	Paul Bailey
Pietro Aretino	*The Secret Life of Nuns*	
Jane Austen	*Lesley Castle*	Zoë Heller
Jane Austen	*Love and Friendship*	Fay Weldon
Honoré de Balzac	*Colonel Chabert*	A.N. Wilson
Charles Baudelaire	*On Wine and Hashish*	Margaret Drabble
Giovanni Boccaccio	*Life of Dante*	A.N. Wilson
Charlotte Brontë	*The Spell*	
Emily Brontë	*Poems of Solitude*	Helen Dunmore
Mikhail Bulgakov	*Fatal Eggs*	Doris Lessing
Mikhail Bulgakov	*The Heart of a Dog*	A.S. Byatt
Giacomo Casanova	*The Duel*	Tim Parks
Miguel de Cervantes	*The Dialogue of the Dogs*	Ben Okri
Geoffrey Chaucer	*The Parliament of Birds*	
Anton Chekhov	*The Story of a Nobody*	Louis de Bernières
Anton Chekhov	*Three Years*	William Fiennes
Wilkie Collins	*The Frozen Deep*	
Joseph Conrad	*Heart of Darkness*	A.N. Wilson
Joseph Conrad	*The Return*	Colm Tóibín
Gabriele D'Annunzio	*The Book of the Virgins*	Tim Parks
Dante Alighieri	*The Divine Comedy: Inferno*	
Dante Alighieri	*New Life*	Louis de Bernières
Daniel Defoe	*The King of Pirates*	Peter Ackroyd
Marquis de Sade	*Incest*	Janet Street-Porter
Charles Dickens	*The Haunted House*	Peter Ackroyd
Charles Dickens	*A House to Let*	
Fyodor Dostoevsky	*The Double*	Jeremy Dyson
Fyodor Dostoevsky	*Poor People*	Charlotte Hobson
Alexandre Dumas	*One Thousand and One Ghosts*	

George Eliot	*Amos Barton*	Matthew Sweet
Henry Fielding	*Jonathan Wild the Great*	Peter Ackroyd
F. Scott Fitzgerald	*The Popular Girl*	Helen Dunmore
Gustave Flaubert	*Memoirs of a Madman*	Germaine Greer
Ugo Foscolo	*Last Letters of Jacopo Ortis*	Valerio Massimo Manfredi
Elizabeth Gaskell	*Lois the Witch*	Jenny Uglow
Théophile Gautier	*The Jinx*	Gilbert Adair
André Gide	*Theseus*	
Johann Wolfgang von Goethe	*The Man of Fifty*	A.S. Byatt
Nikolai Gogol	*The Squabble*	Patrick McCabe
E.T.A. Hoffmann	*Mademoiselle de Scudéri*	Gilbert Adair
Victor Hugo	*The Last Day of a Condemned Man*	Libby Purves
Joris-Karl Huysmans	*With the Flow*	Simon Callow
Henry James	*In the Cage*	Libby Purves
Franz Kafka	*Metamorphosis*	Martin Jarvis
Franz Kafka	*The Trial*	Zadie Smith
John Keats	*Fugitive Poems*	Andrew Motion
Heinrich von Kleist	*The Marquise of O–*	Andrew Miller
Mikhail Lermontov	*A Hero of Our Time*	Doris Lessing
Nikolai Leskov	*Lady Macbeth of Mtsensk*	Gilbert Adair
Carlo Levi	*Words are Stones*	Anita Desai
Xavier de Maistre	*A Journey Around my Room*	Alain de Botton
André Malraux	*The Way of the Kings*	Rachel Seiffert
Katherine Mansfield	*Prelude*	William Boyd
Edgar Lee Masters	*Spoon River Anthology*	Shena Mackay
Guy de Maupassant	*Butterball*	Germaine Greer
Prosper Mérimée	*Carmen*	Philip Pullman
Sir Thomas More	*The History of King Richard III*	Sister Wendy Beckett
Sándor Petőfi	*John the Valiant*	George Szirtes

Francis Petrarch	*My Secret Book*	Germaine Greer
Luigi Pirandello	*Loveless Love*	
Edgar Allan Poe	*Eureka*	Sir Patrick Moore
Alexander Pope	*The Rape of the Lock* and *A Key to the Lock*	Peter Ackroyd
Antoine-François Prévost	*Manon Lescaut*	Germaine Greer
Marcel Proust	*Pleasures and Days*	A.N. Wilson
Alexander Pushkin	*Dubrovsky*	Patrick Neate
Alexander Pushkin	*Ruslan and Lyudmila*	Colm Tóibín
François Rabelais	*Pantagruel*	Paul Bailey
François Rabelais	*Gargantua*	Paul Bailey
Christina Rossetti	*Commonplace*	Andrew Motion
George Sand	*The Devil's Pool*	Victoria Glendinning
Jean-Paul Sartre	*The Wall*	Justin Cartwright
Friedrich von Schiller	*The Ghost-seer*	Martin Jarvis
Mary Shelley	*Transformation*	
Percy Bysshe Shelley	*Zastrozzi*	Germaine Greer
Stendhal	*Memoirs of an Egotist*	Doris Lessing
Robert Louis Stevenson	*Dr Jekyll and Mr Hyde*	Helen Dunmore
Theodor Storm	*The Lake of the Bees*	Alan Sillitoe
Leo Tolstoy	*The Death of Ivan Ilych*	
Leo Tolstoy	*Hadji Murat*	Colm Tóibín
Ivan Turgenev	*Faust*	Simon Callow
Mark Twain	*The Diary of Adam and Eve*	John Updike
Mark Twain	*Tom Sawyer, Detective*	
Oscar Wilde	*The Portrait of Mr W.H.*	Peter Ackroyd
Virginia Woolf	*Carlyle's House and Other Sketches*	Doris Lessing
Virginia Woolf	*Monday or Tuesday*	Scarlett Thomas
Emile Zola	*For a Night of Love*	A.N. Wilson